MW00900486

That Boyce Girl

A NOVEL

R. H. Davis

Compiled and Edited by:
L. H. Davis III

R. H. Davis

ISBN: 1517752752
ISBN 13: 9781517752750
Library of Congress Control Number: 2015916805
CreateSpace Independent Publishing Platform
North Charleston, South Carolina

Dedicated to:

The author, Raymond Harvey Davis, our granduncle

R. H. Davis

The Cover Artist

Laurie Lobaugh Mahoney is a Dallas-based, award-winning artist, website designer – and a grandniece of Raymond Davis. She is a founding member of SLANT, a city-wide artists' collective and a graduate of the Art Institute of Dallas. She has specialized in needle-felted paintings, using natural fiber from sheep, goats, alpaca, and silk worms. Laurie has also recently begun to create works in the stippled pen-and-ink style, which she used for the cover of this book.

A Remembrance

"When I was in the eighth grade we moved to Lutz, Florida from Waycross, Georgia. Betty, my sister, was having health problems and Mother and Daddy thought she would be better off away from the swampy area. My uncle Raymond was living in Lutz and he and Dad built us a small house on his property next to his house. He was a writer, wrote some serials for the newspaper, so not all of the children were allowed in his office when he was working, but I was. I love to read, and we were close, so I spent lots of time reading while he worked. Such a privilege!"

Gloria Davis Lobaugh, Oct. 2015
(Niece of R. H. Davis)

R. H. Davis

Foreword

This novel was written in 1938 by my great-uncle, Raymond Harvey Davis. He wrote this while living in Florida and died there in 1943, at the age of forty-six. He never had children of his own, so not much is known about Raymond, although we do know he served in the U.S. Army during World War I.

That Boyce Girl resides in the public domain, but, unfortunately, I believe I have the only original copy. After drifting through the family for several generations, a very battered manuscript was given to me by Raymond's nephew, my honorable father.

My father did meet Raymond on occasion, back in the 30's, but no one in the family knew Raymond well, most not at all. However, after transcribing this manuscript, one letter at a time, I now feel I do know him, or at least a significant part of him. It's impossible, at least for me, to explain in words why I feel this way, but if you read fiction and claim to have a favorite author . . . I think you understand what I'm trying to say.

I assumed it would take a year or more to transcribe this manuscript, so, while taking breaks from my own writing, I started typing a paragraph or two each night. After sitting all day, I'd stand at my laptop, which I keep on a bar in the kitchen. I refused to read the manuscript in advance, hoping the storyline would force me to keep typing. And the technique worked well; Raymond wrote a page-turner . . . which I had to type in order to turn. I finished transcribing the manuscript after only two months and was sorry to see it end. The storyline hooked me so deeply on that last weekend, I stood and typed for two days in a row, eight hours each day, just so I could find out what happened to Sally, *That Boyce Girl.* And I can tell you, I found it worth the crick in my back . . . and the ach in my feet.

That Boyce Girl is a fun read about that magical period of time in the United States after the Great Depression and before World War II. It was a time when anything was possible, which Raymond captured in living color . . . as he experienced it. *That Boyce Girl* is not a look back in time . . . it unfolds now . . . in 1938.

Sylvester Boyce sold the family home in a desperate attempt to save his faltering bank. Although it was a noble sacrifice, the bank still failed and Sylvester is now bedridden, overcome with grief. To support their family, Sally, Sylvester's young, beautiful, and naive daughter, takes it upon herself to enter the workforce . . . as a car salesman. In 1938, "a woman's place is in the home," but try explaining that to Sally. "Can't" is simply a word she does not understand.

Novels are not easy to write, especially good ones, but Raymond pulled it off. As a writer myself, I couldn't let his work languish, unread on a bookshelf, possibly to eventually be lost forever. If only a single member of our family enjoys this book, now or in the distant future, I know I'll be delighted, and I feel certain Raymond will be, as well. After all, writers . . . write . . . hoping that others will someday read and enjoy their work.

I changed nothing in the manuscript . . . intentionally. I did find a few typos which I corrected. Any spelling errors and typos found within this text now are mine, and I ask for Raymond's forgiveness.

Raymond's style and voice are unique. At first, some of the words and punctuation might feel dated, but within a page or two you'll adapt and sense you're truly back in 1938, which is half the fun. I hope you enjoy adverbs; while writers use them sparingly today, times have definitely changed. Ever heard of "challengingly"? Me neither, but it is a real word. He did use three or four adverbs I couldn't find in the dictionary, but I knew what he meant and so will you.

I hope you enjoy this journey back in time . . . I know I certainly did.

L. H. Davis (Larry)

Bio:
Larry received first place in Florida Writers Association's Royal Palm Literary Awards for his novella *The Emporium* (2011) and again for his sci-fi novel *Outpost Earth* (2013). *The Emporium* was also a semifinalist in the Writers of the Future Contest and has since been

published in the anthology *Swallowed by the Beast.* The Writers of the Future Contest also recognized his short story, *Becoming Eli,* with an honorable mention. Laurance has short stories published in *Aspiring Writers 2014 Winners Anthology* and *A Picture is Worth 1,000 Words.* In July of 2015, his short story, *That Last Summer,* was published on-line in Red Truck Review's third literary journal.

Other books in this series by L. H. Davis:

The Race: That Boyce Girl 1939

The Murder of Miss Shelby Putnam: That Boyce Girl 1940

CHAPTER 1

A Resounding Smack

Sally Boyce stopped for a moment before the entrance to the Ulmer Motor Sales Company, feeling the temptation to turn and run.

Then her thoughts conjured up a picture of her father, lying so quietly in bed, staring hopelessly at the ceiling—and the temptation was gone.

Red lips firm, shoulders erect, Sally marched through the entrance and into the display room. She felt a little braver as her glance moved over the highly polished cars there.

A young man came to meet her. He had sandy hair, wide shoulders and steady blue eyes, but with a reckless glint in their depths.

"I'm Jeff Rainey, one of Philip Ulmer's salesmen," he introduced himself, smiling. His eyes widened a little. "Aren't you Miss Sally Boyce?"

"Yes, I'm Sally Boyce. I want to see Mr. Ulmer."

"We've just received the new Duluth roadster, Miss Boyce. I feel sure you will want one."

Sally's smile was rueful as she shook her head.

"I want to see Mr. Ulmer, please."

Jeff looked faintly puzzled. "Won't take but a moment to show you the new roadster," he persisted.

Sally thought that his face looked familiar, but she couldn't place him, and, of course, had no desire to.

Jeff's eyes were twinkling. "I've seen you at the country club several times, but I don't believe you saw me."

Sally could understand that. For two years now, she had been blind to every man but Walter Norris.

"I came to see Mr. Ulmer about a job," she explained coolly. "I've decided that I want to sell Duluth cars."

Jeff's eyes widened. "You? Sell Duluths!"

Sally found his amazement rather insulting. "Is there any reason why a girl shouldn't sell automobiles?" she said stiffly.

Jeff studied her for a moment, shrugged. "You might get away with it at that."

Sally moved past him, but Jeff turned and went with her. He opened the door to Philip Ulmer's office.

"I'll stay here," Jeff whispered, grinning, "so that I can catch you when Ulmer throws you out."

Sally ignored him pointedly. She managed a smile for the benefit of the plump little man who rose from behind his desk to greet her. Her heart was beating faster now. She knew that Ulmer's smile would vanish when she stated her errand.

"Good morning, Miss Boyce. Did Jeff show you the new roadster?"

Sally touched her tongue to her dry lips. "He tried to, but I'm looking for a job, Mr. Ulmer. I— I want to sell Duluths."

Philip Ulmer's smile remained intact; his expression said that he appreciated her little joke.

"It's true," Sally said earnestly. "I've owned two of them, and I know what a grand car it is."

Ulmer was obviously puzzled.

"Why do you want to sell cars, Miss Boyce?"

Sally sighed helplessly. Everybody in Avondale knew that the Citizens Bank had closed its doors six months ago, but none of them believed that Sylvester Boyce had actually used every dollar of his own fortune in an effort to stave off that disaster.

"I must make a living," Sally said quietly. "For my parents and for myself."

She saw in Ulmer's eyes the dubious look she had seen so many times during the past six months. It said plainly that bankers didn't go broke along with their banks. It said that, while they might move from their mansions to small houses on the wrong side of town, this was just a ruse to allay suspicion.

"How is your father, Miss Boyce?" Ulmer asked.

"Dad isn't any better," Sally replied, and her throat was tight with pity and love for the man who had gone down to defeat.

Ulmer stared at her thoughtfully. He saw a girl of 20, with wide brown eyes and bronze-brown hair, a tea rose complexion. He thought that she would look very lovely at the wheel of a Duluth. "So, you want to sell Duluths?" he murmured doubtfully.

Sally's voice trembled. "I'm sure that I could sell them!"

Ulmer's gaze met hers squarely. "Is it really necessary for you to work?"

Sally stated the truth bluntly. "My mother sold the jewelry she owned before she married Dad, but the money is gone now and I must earn some more."

"You know the right kind of people," Ulmer admitted, "but I've never used a girl salesman."

He shook his head, frowning. "Selling cars is hard work, Miss Boyce. Surely your friends can find something easier for you."

"I don't want something easier," Sally said determinedly. "I want to show this town that the Boyces aren't whipped yet."

"But you don't know anything about selling."

Smiling, Sally quoted the slogan which was famous the country over: "'The Duluth Sells Itself.'"

Ulmer's eyes twinkled faintly. "A good slogan, but we find that it doesn't take the place of persistent effort."

"I'll be persistent," Sally promised eagerly.

Ulmer studied her face a moment longer, then pressed a button on his desk and a girl appeared from an adjoining office.

"Send Jeff in here," Ulmer ordered then looked at Sally as the girl disappeared. "I have nothing to lose, so I'll give you a chance. Straight commission, no drawing account."

Sally was unable to speak for a moment. She hadn't dared believe that it would be so easy. "You mean I can sell Duluths?" she gasped.

"I mean that you can try," Ulmer said dryly. "I'm going to turn you over to Jeff Rainey. He'll show you the new Duluth and give you whatever instructions you need."

Sally's heart was singing and not even the presence of Jeff Rainey beside her could make the future seem anything but bright. Since they had left Ulmer's in a Duluth roadster, Jeff had been mentioning the finer points of the car.

"And now you can forget all that," he said abruptly. "It doesn't mean a thing in the world."

Sally had been listening attentively and looked at him now. "What do you mean?"

Everything I've told you about the Duluth is true of most cars of its price class," Jeff explained, smiling. "If you want to sell Duluths, you must use your natural talents."

"I intend to work hard," Sally said firmly.

Jeff shook his head, grinning. "You should call on men prospects. Just wave those long eyelashes at them, and they'll buy."

Sally breathed angrily. "I'll do nothing of the sort!"

Jeff shrugged. "You will, if you're smart." Then he asked, "Is your father feeling any better?"

"He's still very sick," Sally replied, and watched Jeff's face for the cynical look she had learned to expect. But it didn't appear.

"I know your father," he said quietly.

"I suppose you lost your life's savings," Sally said bitterly, "and that you blame it all on Dad?"

"I lost a little but I don't blame it on anybody," Jeff said.

"That's kind of you."

"You might tell him that I plan to visit him soon."

"His doctor doesn't allow visitors," she said, and then her curiosity got the best of her. "What do you want to see him about?"

"Business," Jeff said briefly, grinning. He made a U-turn at the next cross street, and then they were headed toward town again. "How would you like to sell a Duluth today?"

"I— I don't know," she quavered.

"You can't learn any younger," Jeff said, and frowned thoughtfully. "Do you know Adolph Gingrich?"

Sally shivered. She didn't know the man personally, but she did know that he had lost heavily through her father's bank. "I'd rather call on someone else," she said uneasily.

Jeff glanced at her, frowning. "You can't depend on the country club crowd, alone. They're all right, but there aren't enough of them."

"It isn't that," Sally said, flushing. "I think I'd rather call on a woman first."

"Women prefer to buy from men," Jeff said, his eyes twinkling. "Please remember what I told you about your natural talents."

Sally looked away from his amused, admiring gaze. She couldn't admit to this irritating young man that she was afraid to see Gingrich, afraid of what he might say about her father.

"I'm willing to call on Mr. Gingrich," she said calmly, and prayed that the man would not realize who she was.

Jeff drove silently for some moments, then he asked, "Aren't you engaged to Walter Norris?"

Sally's eyes fell to the diamond ring on her finger. It had rested there since Walter came home from college two years ago and went to work in her father's bank. But Walter's job and most of his mother's money had disappeared when the bank collapsed; and now Walter was trying without much success to sell insurance.

"Yes, I'm engaged to him," she said, and wondered how many dreary years would pass before they could afford to be married.

Jeff turned a corner and then another, and they were in the wholesale district of Avondale.

"You should forget about the bank," he told her. "Some people think your father is dishonest, others think that he is honest. Since you can't do anything to change their opinions, you should forget about it."

Sally gave him a resentful glance. "I intend to prove to everybody that Dad is honest," she said firmly.

"That's a pretty big job for a small girl with red hair."

"It isn't red—" Sally began angrily.

The car slid to the curb before a one-story brick building. A big sign across the front of it said, "Adolf Gingrich Wholesale Plumbing Company."

Sally was trembling as she walked with Jeff Rainey toward the entrance. Jeff's hand on her arm steadied her.

"He won't bite—not more than once," Jeff said cheerfully. He opened the door. "I'll let you do most of the talking . . . but don't forget your eyelashes."

A huge, thick-shouldered man in a loud suit looked up at them from behind a scarred desk. He gave Jeff a friendly nod.

"Still selling cars, Jeff?"

Jeff admitted that he was; then he introduced Sally and stated their mission. But the big man was staring at Sally now, and his face was no longer genial.

"Miss Sally Boyce?" he repeated, frowning. He rose from his chair and circled the desk. "Are you any kin to Sylvester Boyce?"

Sally met that frowning gaze steadily. "Sylvester Boyce is my father," she said proudly.

Gingrich's face was suffused with red. "You've got your nerve coming here. Your old man stole ten thousand dollars from me!"

A wave of anger swept over Sally. That red face before her represented the faces of all the Avondale people who had slandered her father.

The man was repeating the accusation when Sally's hand smacked resoundingly against his cheek, stopping his voice, bringing a dazed look to his eyes.

Wide shoulders slipped between Sally and the plumber.

"Maybe you'd like to quarrel with me, too, Gingrich?" Jeff Rainey purred invitingly.

Scowling, Gingrich circled the desk again, sank into his chair.

"Get out—both of you!" he snarled.

Sally felt the sick pounding of her heart. She could picture Philip Ulmer's resentment when he learned of this, could almost hear his angry voice as he fired her. In attempting to defend her father, she had failed him.

CHAPTER 2

Men with Money

When Sally reached home that night, she was still finding it hard to believe that she had not been fired. But Jeff Rainey had explained the Adolph Gingrich incident to Philip Ulmer, and Ulmer had merely looked thoughtful and advised her not to make a practice of slapping people, if she expected to sell automobiles.

Sally found her mother lying on a sofa in the small living room, her gray hair damp from the heat, her thin face pale. She sat up, sighing, as Sally entered the room.

"I haven't cooked supper yet," Mrs. Boyce said in a tired voice. "It's been so dreadfully hot."

"I got a job today," Sally said proudly.

"A job!" Mrs. Boyce gasped. "What do mean, Sally?"

Sally told her everything, expecting her to look relieved. But Mrs. Boyce's lips quivered.

It's ridiculous," Mrs. Boyce said fretfully. "I simply won't allow it."

"But our money is almost gone," Sally pointed out. "I had to do something."

Mrs. Boyce's thin hands were locked nervously in her lap.

"What will our friends think when they learn about this?" she moaned.

Sally sank down beside her and put a comforting arm around her.

"We don't have to worry about the opinions of our friends," Sally said with a wry smile. "Most of them think very badly of us anyway."

"If Sylvester hadn't been such a fool," Mrs. Boyce said in a choking voice, "this would not have happened."

Sally rose to her feet, fighting to keep her anger in check. "Dad did what was right," she said quietly. "The only thing that makes life bearable is our knowledge that he did not betray his friends, that he lost everything while trying to save them. Dad was like the captain of a ship, choosing to go down with his vessel. I'm proud of him!" But Sally knew that it was useless, knew that her mother would always resent her husband's action. Mrs. Boyce had collapsed when he told her that he had spent his personal fortune in that vain effort to save his bank.

"You must not worry about it, Mother," Sally said huskily. "I don't mind working."

Mrs. Boyce raised a hopeless face. "You know nothing whatever about business, Sally. You can't hope to sell automobiles."

Sally looked away from her mother, shivering as she recalled her encounter with Adolph Gingrich. She knew that most of Avondale shared Gingrich's opinion of her father, knew that she would meet up with the same difficulty again and again. "I haven't sold a car yet," Sally admitted. "But I will, Mother. I must!"

Mrs. Boyce sighed. "You are being very foolish, dear. There is only one course for you to follow."

"What is that, Mother?"

"You must get married."

"But Walter and I can't be married now," Sally protested. "He isn't making enough money."

Mrs. Boyce's lips tightened. "Has Walter mentioned marriage since he lost his job at the bank?"

"Walter is looking for a better job," Sally said defensively. "When he gets it, we will be married.

"Walter isn't the only man in Avondale," Mrs. Boyce said sharply. "There are other men, fine men—men with money."

"But Walter and I love each other," Sally said quietly. "Surely you wouldn't want me to marry a man simply because we need money?"

Ready tears came to Mrs. Boyce's eyes. "I want anything that will get us out of this horrible little house, anything that will permit us to live like human beings again."

That desperate voice rang in Sally's ears as she moved toward the door. "You lie down again, Mother," Sally ordered gently. "I'll get supper."

A supper-laden tray in her hands, Sally stopped just outside her father's bedroom door, bracing herself. Remembering him as he had been—jovial and kindly, sure of himself and of his ability—it was heartbreaking to see him as he was now. Balancing the tray carefully, smiling cheerfully, Sally moved into the room and placed the tray on a small bedside table. "Hungry Dad?"

Sylvester Boyce's gray head turned on the pillow. Dull eyes peered at her from beneath shaggy eyebrows.

"No, I'm not hungry, Sally."

Sally wagged a reproving finger at him. "But you must eat, young man. You'll never recover your strength unless you eat lots of nourishing food."

"I'm so much bother to you and Mother," he sighed.

She told him about her job at Ulmer's and he looked at her, frowning.

"But why are you going to work? I thought you were going to marry Walter."

"Walter and I have decided to postpone our wedding," Sally evaded. "I've always wanted to get a job."

Sylvester Boyce looked vaguely troubled. "I want you to be married, dear. It's the only way for a girl to be happy." His eyes showed a little animation. "Doesn't Jeff Rainey work at Ulmer's, Sally?"

Sally bit her lip. Jeff Rainey had been kind to her; she even suspected that he had saved her job. But Jeff had a blunt manner of speech that irritated her. "Yes, Jeff works there, Dad," she replied, and was amazed to see a faint sparkle in her father's eyes. Those eyes that had been so dull for six months.

"Did Jeff tell you about his ideas?" he asked.

"No, he didn't"

"I'll be well soon," Sylvester Boyce whispered dully. "Then we'll move back to our old house and have plenty of money."

Sally lifted the tray and prepared to leave. His words were brave enough, but his hopeless tone told her that he never expected to be well again, never expected to recoup his fortunes. "I know you will, Dad," she said stoutly, and was able to hold back the tears until she had reached her own room. Then she remembered that Walter was taking her to the country club that night and hurriedly bathed and dressed.

~ ~ ~

As they drove away from the house that night, Walter Norris smiled at Sally. “You’re looking particularly lovely tonight, darling.”

Sally returned that tender smile. It was good to be with him again, for he was all that remained out of the old life. “No matter what else changes,” she thought, “our love will endure.”

“I phoned you this afternoon,” Walter was saying. “Your mother said that you were down town.”

Sally was reminded of her good news and wondered why she dreaded telling it. Walter must know that it was necessary, and his love for her would give him understanding. “I went to town and got myself a job,” she burst out.

Walter was silent as he guided the car around a corner, then he glanced at her and his dark eyes were curious. “You must be joking, Sally.”

Sally looked at the road ahead. Walter called her darling when he was pleased, Sally when he wasn’t. “I’m going to sell Duluth cars, Walter. I started today, but of course I haven’t sold one yet.”

Walter was silent again until the town fell behind them and the county highway opened up ahead. “I don’t like it,” he said flatly.

Sally looked at him, seeing the dark curls tumbled over his forehead, the regular profile. But the handsome mouth she loved was sullen now. She put a hand on his arm eager for his understanding. “It was necessary for me to get a job, dear. We are at the end of our resources and I must earn some money.”

Walter glanced at her, his dark eyebrows raised. “I find that hard to believe, Sally.”

Sally met his eyes bravely. “We have only a few dollars left, and it’s up to me to earn more.”

“Do you mean to say that your father made no provisions for your mother?” Walter demanded.

They had never discussed this before, but she realized now that Walter shared the town’s belief that Sylvester Boyce had feathered his own nest at the expense of the people who trusted him. “Mother had some jewelry before she married Dad,” Sally said dully. “We have been living on the money we got for that, but the money is almost gone, now."

"I just can't believe it," Walter muttered.

"But it is true," Sally insisted. "Dad couldn't have done anything else. He owed a duty to all those people who had trusted him with their money."

The brakes squealed as Walter brought the roadster to a stop at the side of the road. He turned to her frowning. "Your father also owed a duty to you and your mother. Are you sure that he has no money?"

"I am quite sure," Sally replied. "Dad turned everything we owned over to the bank's creditors—money, house, furniture, cars—everything."

Walter shook his head. "You must tell your father tomorrow that you have no money. If he has none, then he can borrow it."

"It isn't true," Sally said stiffly. "The Boyce family has neither money nor credit." But Sally realized, as he drew her into his arms, that he didn't believe it, and her lips were cold under his. He released her in a moment, and his mouth looked determined.

"Let's get married at once, Sally. We love each other, and we must not wait any longer."

CHAPTER 3

Gary's Genial Smile

Sally's heart melted at Walter's words. For six months she had waited for him to speak again of their marriage, had suspected at times that he regretted their engagement. But now, he was asking her to marry him at once—and life was worth living again. She let him kiss her again then pushed him away, but feeling the urge to bury her face against his shoulder and agree. "We can't be married yet, Walter," she said huskily.

Walter's teasing eyes said that he wasn't taking her refusal seriously. "I have enough money to buy the license and pay the minister, Sally. We can trust to luck for the rest."

Sally felt an impulse to cast caution to the four winds, to do what her heart and Walter demanded. She took his hand and hugged it against her breast. "We'll have to wait, Walter, but it's worth waiting for."

"I've been waiting, hoping to make more money," Walter said impatiently. "I'm beginning to believe that it's a futile hope."

"But I have to take care of Dad and Mother," Sally explained. "I'll always have to take care of them."

Again, Walter refused to take her seriously. "Imagine a baby like you trying to earn a living."

"I haven't any choice," Sally replied, feeling resentful. "We must have a roof over our heads and food on the table and medicines for Dad."

"You've allowed yourself to become panic-stricken," Walter said impatiently. "You haven't given your problems time to work themselves out."

"My problems are becoming more numerous every day," Sally said soberly. "That's why I got a job."

Walter's handsome face fell into petulant lines. "You are being stubborn, Sally. This job of yours is just a gesture. You know nothing of business."

"I'm sorry I seem so stupid to you," Sally said resentfully.

"That isn't the question," he said sulkily. "It's a matter of business training, which you lack."

Hoping to put him in a good humor again, Sally told him about her experiences of the day, including the one with Adolph Gingrich.

"You slapped a plumber?" Walter breathed angrily.

"He said that Dad was dishonest and so I slapped him. I'm glad that I did."

Walter's mouth set grimly. "You are not to go back to Ulmer's tomorrow morning, Sally."

Sally hardly heard him; she had thought of a way out of their difficulty. "We could get married," she said in a small voice, "if you would let me go on working."

Walter shook his head. "We can be married now, but I can't permit you to work. What do you think my mother, and all our friends, will say?"

"Lots of married girls work," Sally evaded his question. "Nobody thinks anything about it anymore."

"I won't have a working wife," Walter said stubbornly. "I want you to ask your father tomorrow if he hasn't made some provision for you and your mother."

"I can't ask him such a question," Sally said angrily. "He would consider it an insult, and I would agree with him."

"Is it a crime to provide a living for your wife and daughter?" Walter asked querulously.

Sally remained silent. She suspected that Walter, like her own mother, would never understand Sylvester Boyce's actions.

"Did you say that you were with Jeff Rainey today, Sally?"

Sally nodded. "He was very kind to me."

"I don't want you to know people like Jeff," Walter growled. "I went to high school with him and he's just a roughneck full of half-baked ideas. Promise me that you won't go back to Ulmer's tomorrow."

"I must go back there tomorrow," Sally said firmly.

The gears clashed as Walter threw the car in motion; and an unpleasant silence held them until they reached the country club.

~ ~ ~

Sally had danced a dozen times and was seeing other men for the first time since she had fallen in love with Walter. But she was merely seeing them as possible buyers of Duluth cars. She had told each of her dance partners about her new job.

Gary Neylands tapped her partner's shoulder, and Sally smiled at him as she went into his arms. Gary was about 35, with dark sleek hair and wise grey eyes. He was a manufacturer of automobile accessories; and a perfect example of the successful young businessman.

"I've been hearing things about you, Sally," Gary said with a genial smile.

Sally had always known that Gary more than liked her, but she had known it in an uncaring way. "Perhaps you have heard about my new job," she smiled.

Gary nodded, his grey eyes sober. "I think you are very brave, Sally. Most of the girls in your set wouldn't have the courage to do what you've done."

Sally felt warmed by his words. Gary was a self-made man and his praise meant something. "I do hope I will make good," Sally said earnestly.

"I believe that you will," Gary replied. Then his eyes swept the crowded dance floor. "Most of your friends believe that the Boyces still have money, Sally. Some of them won't be so friendly when they learn the truth."

Sally was both drawn and repelled by his tone. She was remembering gossip she had heard—that Gary Neylands was not too scrupulous in his business affairs.

"I'm one of those who know the truth," Gary continued quietly, "and I still think that you are a grand person."

Sally quickly changed the subject from that of a personal nature. "You wouldn't happen to be in the market for a car, would you?" she asked gaily. Gary laughed with her, but Sally was conscious of the tightening of his arm about her.

"Oddly enough, I am," he said.

Sally found it hard to breathe. "You mean you really want to buy a car?"

"I really do," Gary said, smiling at what he saw in her face. Then he asked, "Could you manage to show me a Duluth tomorrow?"

"Could I show you a Duluth tomorrow!" Sally whispered ecstatically. "Oh, just couldn't I!"

"I'll be pretty busy all day," Gary said. "Perhaps we could combine business with a luncheon?"

Sally hesitated for only a moment. She knew that Walter wouldn't approve, but selling a Duluth was so important. And so she agreed.

"Then bring a car to my plant at noon," Gary continued. "By the way, what is the price of the Duluth sedan?"

"I'm not sure about the prices," she explained. "But I'll find out in the morning."

Gary shrugged. "The price isn't important."

When that dance ended, Sally slipped away to the dressing room and there she found Louise Ives, beautiful but rather spoiled daughter of a wealthy Avondale family. Sally usually avoided Louise, knowing that the girl was in love with Walter.

"I hear you have gone into business, Sally," Louise said with a malicious smile.

"Yes, I'm selling Duluth cars," Sally admitted, still thrilled by the thought that she had practically sold one to Gary Neylands.

"What's the big idea?" Louise asked bluntly.

"To make a living," Sally replied.

"Has your father cut off your allowance?" Louise persisted.

"I haven't had one for six months," Sally said quietly.

"Really!" Louise sneered; then her eyes brightened. "I'll bet Walter doesn't approve of you working."

Sally shrugged and turned to a dressing table. She didn't want to discuss Walter or the Boyce finances with Louise, fearing the girl might say something she would regret.

"I've always wanted Walter," Louise said suddenly, "and I think this is a good time to get him."

Sally turned to the girl, too amazed to speak. Louise was notoriously outspoken, but she had never seen her like this. "You don't realize what you are saying," Sally said quietly.

Louise glared at her. "I know what I'm saying, and I mean every word of it.

Sally made the necessary repairs on her makeup, then moved toward the door.

Louise's jeering voice followed her. "My father was careful to put his money in the right bank, Sally—and Walter Norris is no fool!"

~ ~ ~

They left the dance early, at Sally's insistence; and on the way home she told Walter the good news. "I've sold a car!" she said happily. "If I can do that well every day, I'll soon be rich."

"Who did you sell a car to?" Walter asked, frowning.

"Well, I didn't exactly sell one," Sally admitted, conscious that Walter was not pleased. "But I made an appointment to show a sedan to Gary Neylands tomorrow." She expected him to show anger for he had expressed his poor opinion of Gary many times in the past.

"Oh, Gary Neylands," Walter said, and his face cleared.

Sally was surprised, but elated, by the change in his expression. "I feel sure that he will buy one," she said gaily.

Walter looked away from her. "Gary is trying to find a place for me at his plant, Sally. I don't much like the fellow, but I've got to get out of the insurance business. I just can't sell the stuff."

"I think that something else will turn up," she said hopefully.

When they drew to a stop in front of her house, Sally stared curiously at the new Duluth car parked just ahead of them. "I wonder who it is?" she said, and glanced toward the house to find that the lights were still burning upstairs and down.

"Might be Dr. Frobisher, calling on your father," Walter suggested.

"He calls on Dad in the morning, and he doesn't drive a Duluth," Sally replied, and then her heart sank. "Maybe it's Philip Ulmer, come to fire me."

"I certainly hope so!" Walter said fervently.

CHAPTER 4

Breathless

Mrs. Boyce looked up from her book as Sally entered the living room. "Did you have a nice time at the country club?"

Sally nodded, breathing a sigh of relief. She had expected to find Philip Ulmer there, waiting to tell her she was fired. Then it occurred to her that he might be upstairs with her father. "Is Dad having a visitor?" Sally asked uneasily.

Mrs. Boyce frowned. "He's been with your father for two hours. I don't know what to make of it."

"Who is it?"

"A Mr. Jeff Rainey, and I must say that he has poor manners. I told him your father could see no visitors, but he just grinned at me and went on upstairs."

"I've been up there twice, trying to get rid of him," Mrs. Boyce complained. "But your father won't let him go. I can't imagine what has come over Sylvester."

"Mr. Rainey has been kind to me, and he doesn't mean any harm," Sally told her. "I'll get rid of him."

Sally found her father's bedroom door open, and her eyes went first to him. Sylvester Boyce was propped up in bed, his thin face flushed. Her angry eyes went to Jeff Rainey, who twisted about in his chair and smiled at her.

"Hello, Sally."

Sally moved into the room. "You know you shouldn't be awake so late, Dad," she said reprovingly.

"It's good for a man to stay up late once in a while," Jeff Rainey commented lightly.

Sally gave him a resentful glance. "Perhaps you know more about it than Dr. Frobisher."

Jeff looked irritatingly amiable. "Perhaps," he agreed.

Sally glanced at her father. "Dr. Frobisher told you to be careful, Dad."

"I've been having a very entertaining evening," her father said gently. "Jeff has been telling me about his ideas. Some of them are very good."

"Only some of them?" Jeff complained, smiling.

Sylvester Boyce looked at Sally. "Jeff has an invention for inflating tires while the car is in motion, through compressed air from the engine. Ought to be big money in it."

His flushed face worried Sally. For months now he had stared hopelessly at the ceiling, showing no interest in anything. But he was obviously excited now, and she feared it might hurt him. "My father is in no condition to discuss business, Mr. Rainey," she said stiffly.

"You may call me Jeff," Jeff said blandly; then he frowned at her. "It'll be good for your father to talk about business."

Sally's voice trembled slightly. "Dr. Frobisher has expressly forbidden it! Where did you meet my father?"

"I used to go into the bank to tell him about my ideas," Jeff told her. "I first met him when I was a kid, selling papers on the street. He always gave me a quarter and told me to keep the change."

Sally remembered Walter's indictment of Jeff and found that she could not agree with it. Jeff Rainey was an irritating person, but he was definitely not a roughneck. "Very interesting," she said lightly.

Jeff's eyes twinkled. "I expect to make lots of money out of my ideas. From newsboy to millionaire."

Sylvester Boyce chuckled. "Jeff told me about your encounter with Adolph Gingrich. It was very amusing."

Sally frowned at Jeff. *A sick man shouldn't be told such things.*

Jeff's big body rose from his chair, and Mr. Boyce murmured a protest. "Must you go, Jeff?"

Jeff shook his head. "I'm afraid so," he said.

"Then come back soon," Mr. Boyce said. "I'm interested in your plans."

"Dr. Frobisher has said that you must not have visitors," Sally protested.

"Women and doctors!" Jeff sniffed, and headed for the door.

Sally followed him, trembling with anger. She couldn't speak her mind before her father, but Jeff should not leave here without learning what she thought of his conduct. Jeff was going swiftly down the stairs, apparently unaware that she was following him; and that, too, was irritating. Jeff called a cheery goodnight to her mother, grabbed his hat from a rack in the hall and strode through the front door.

"Oh, Mr. Rainey!" Sally called, out of breath.

Jeff turned, obviously surprised and just as obviously not particularly pleased to see her. "Did I forget something, Sally?"

"I must ask you not to visit my father again," she said coldly. "His doctor doesn't allow it."

"Your father needs a new interest in life, Sally. It'll be good for him to see me, occasionally."

Sally's fingers curled. "I must ask you not to come here again," she flared.

"I came to see your father—not you," Jeff said, grinning.

Sally's nails dug into her palms. "You shouldn't have told him about Gingrich. It might have worried him."

"But it didn't." Jeff's smile vanished. "I did forget something, Sally. I forgot to kiss you goodnight."

Sally's stepped back, but she was too late. Jeff's big hands were at her waist, lifting her. His mouth met hers, bruising her lips. He set her down, and Sally put all her strength in her flying hand.

Jeff rubbed his cheek; his eyes were admiring. "You pack quite a wallop, Sally."

"You hateful impudent!"

~ ~ ~

When Sally went to work the next morning, she saw Jeff on the display floor showing a Duluth roadster to a ravishing blond, who seemed to be more interested in Jeff than in the car. Sally made her face contemptuous, but Jeff didn't glance in her direction, which gave fresh fuel to her wrath. She went on to Ulmer's office, wanting to get a price-list and to tell him about Gary Neylands. But she found Ulmer dictating to his secretary, and he had only enough time to tell her to see Jeff about anything she wanted to know. Sally returned to the display floor and sat down in a chair. Presently Jeff and the blond moved past her, and Sally heard the woman agree to buy the car.

"But only on condition that you teach me to drive it," the woman gushed.

"Be a pleasure," Jeff replied amiably, "and now we'll go to the office and sign on the dotted line."

Sally looked after them and saw the woman's admiring eyes raised to Jeff. Jeff had one hand at her elbow, guiding her toward the office—and the dotted line. Sally sniffed. *Blonds! Sandy haired men who kissed girls against their will!* She had a poor opinion of both.

Jeff was back presently, but he gave Sally a blank glance. "Did you want to look at a Duluth, Madam?" he inquired politely.

Sally rose to her feet, staring at him coldly. "Mr. Ulmer told me to get a price-list from you."

Jeff's eyes widened. "Well, if it isn't Sally Boyce, our new salesman! Or is it saleslady?"

"A price-list, please," Sally said stiffly.

Jeff found one in his pocket, gave it to her. "Mad about something, Sally?"

Sally glared at him. "I don't like to be kissed."

Jeff appeared perplexed. "Who kissed you?"

"You did!" Sally snapped.

Jeff's face was a picture of amazement. "Are you sure?" he murmured. "I don't seem to remember it." His wide shoulders lifted. "A kiss isn't important, so don't act red-headed about it."

Sally turned her back on him and marched toward the street door. Jeff's hand on her arm brought her to a stop, and she wheeled on him, her eyes blazing.

"They're polishing a car for you in the repair shop. I'll bring it around front for you." Jeff's voice was crisply businesslike. "You can't sell a Duluth unless you demonstrate them."

~ ~ ~

Lunching with Gary Neylands, Sally was both pleased and perplexed by his attitude. She was pleased because he seemed to be in a good humor and because she felt that he intended to buy a Duluth. But she was perplexed by what she saw in his eyes. While his lips uttered banalities, his eyes said something else—that he liked her more than he dared say at present.

"Are you enjoying your lunch, Sally?" Gary asked, his admiring eyes on her flushed face.

"Very much," Sally smiled, and it was true enough. The food was delicious, and she had a handsome and successful luncheon partner. One who intended to buy a Duluth!

Gary sounded amused. "You look very thoughtful, Sally."

"If you buy a Duluth, it will be my first sale," Sally explained, with a tremulous smile. "Naturally, I'm excited about it."

"Don't let it spoil your lunch," Gary advised, smiling.

But Sally found it hard to force even small bites past the huge lump in her throat. And she was breathless with excitement as they left the restaurant and entered the Duluth she had parked at the curb. "Where shall I drive you, Gary?" Sally asked.

"Couldn't we go to the country club and play a round of golf?" Gary asked.

Sally felt uneasy suddenly. Was he using this demonstration merely as an excuse to be with her, or did he actually intend to buy? "I can't take the afternoon off," she explained. "I might lose my job."

"Then drive me anywhere you like, Sally. I'll enjoy it, no matter where we go."

But he sounded rather hurt, and Sally wondered if she had ruined her chances of selling him a Duluth? The thought made her shiver. It was so dreadfully necessary to earn some money!

CHAPTER 5

Bewildered

Sally's doubts vanished as she drove along a country road with Gary Neylands. The Duluth was purring like a kitten, freshly gorged with cream. And Gary had had some complimentary things to say about the car. "It's a wonderful car!" Sally said enthusiastically. "I've owned two of them myself."

"It's a shame you can't still have a car of your own," Gary said quietly.

Sally shrugged. "I don't mind walking. I just want to be sure to earn enough money for food and rent and medicines for Dad."

"Your father is a remarkable person, Sally. Not one banker in a hundred would beggar himself trying to save his depositors."

Sally warmed to his words, then found herself wondering if Gary would have done the same, and if he really did admire her father. And chided herself for the thought.

"Has Walter told you that I'm going to find a place for him at the plant?" Gary asked presently.

Sally nodded, smiling. "Walter is so pleased about it. He hates selling insurance."

"I can understand that," Gary said sympathetically. "Walter is the executive type. He could never make good at selling."

Sally's doubts were alive again. She couldn't believe that Gary really meant this, because Walter was so plainly not the executive type. She had an uneasy feeling that Gary was merely trying to please her, and so she turned at the next crossroad and headed for the city, again. "I mustn't keep you away from your office too long," she explained, smiling.

"Please don't hurry on my account," Gary protested. "It's a relief to get away from business cares occasionally. I'm giving a dinner party at my country place Saturday night," Gary was saying. "I'd like for you to come, Sally."

Sally looked straight ahead. Was he inviting her, alone, to his country place? Was this the price he expected her to pay, if he was to purchase a car from her?

"I phoned Walter about it this morning," Gary continued. "He said he would have to speak to you about it."

Sally let out a relieved breath, hating herself for her suspicion. "Why, yes. We'd be glad to go, Gary." She had an uneasy feeling that Gary had noticed her hesitation, and that he knew its reason. She felt color stealing into her face.

"I had a small party in mind, Sally. You and Walter, Jeff Rainey and Carol Putnam, Louise Ives and myself. One gets so bored with the country club and the usual places, and I thought you might like a change."

"It sounds very nice, Gary," she replied, wishing that he hadn't made it sound so personal.

"If you don't like any of these people, I'll invite someone else. I want you to be pleased."

"I like all of them," Sally said quickly, and felt that she was being fairly truthful. She didn't really dislike Louise Ives, in spite of the girl's outrageous remarks at the country club last night. And the word was much too mild to express her feelings for Jeff Rainey.

"I suppose you've met Jeff Rainey at Ulmer's," Gary said casually.

"Yes," Sally said in a controlled voice, "I've met him."

Gary laughed a little. "You sound as if you aren't one of Jeff's admirers."

"I scarcely know him."

"Jeff is an odd character," Gary said thoughtfully. "He has good ideas but he doesn't carry them to a logical conclusion. So many men have that fault, and it keeps them from becoming successful."

"Jeff expects to become a millionaire," Sally said lightly.

"I doubt that," Gary laughed, "but he could do very well, if he could be persuaded to listen to reason."

Sally felt bewildered. She had taken Jeff Rainey and his ideas rather lightly, but it seemed that Gary Neylands and her father thought well of both.

"I've decided to interest myself in Jeff's inventions," Gary told her. "If I can persuade him to turn them over to me and let my experts perfect them. I'll make Jeff a well-to-do young man."

"Jeff was talking to Dad last night about some of his ideas," she told Gary.

"Indeed!" Gary exclaimed. "Do you remember what Jeff Said?"

Sally searched her memory and the search made her cheeks burn. She didn't like to be reminded of Jeff Rainey. She wanted quickly to forget everything he had said and done. But she remembered suddenly what her father had told her. "Jeff has an invention for inflating tires while the car is in motion, through compressed air from the engine." She laughed scornfully. "It doesn't sound very sensible to me." She was conscious of Gary's excitement, conscious of the tremor in his voice.

"It's funny that no one thought of that before. It would make a million dollars—if he can do it."

Sally resented his excitement, resented his admiration for Jeff's idea, and wondered why she should resent them. Jeff had kissed her but he hadn't been serious about it, so there was no reason why she should hate him so. She thought of her father, as she had seen him before going to work that morning. She wondered if Jeff's visit was responsible for Mr. Boyce's brighter eyes, his stronger voice? She shook her head. It just wasn't reasonable.

"Did Jeff mention any of the details of his invention?" Gary asked quietly.

"I don't remember any," Sally replied. "But he may have told Dad more about it."

"Has Jeff patented it?" Gary persisted. "Or is he merely working on the idea?"

"I don't know," Sally replied, and was pleased to see the Neylands plant just ahead. The huge glass-and-steel building covered several acres of ground, and the air vibrated to its machinery.

Gary smiled at her as the Duluth came to a stop before the entrance. "If you will come with me to my office, we can conclude our business, Sally," Gary said.

In Gary's wide, high-ceilinged office, Sally sat in a chair and watched with shining eyes as he filled out a check. His scratching pen sounded like celestial music in her ears. "My first sale!" she thought ecstatically. Gary blotted the check and handed it to her. Sally put it in her bag, unable to speak. She rose to her feet.

"I'll send someone for the car, Sally. You can tell Ulmer to mail me a bill-of-sale." He rose, smiling. "Don't forget that you are coming to my country place Saturday night."

"I won't forget, Gary—and thanks for the nice luncheon and for buying a car from me."

Gary shrugged away her thanks. "Tell your father that I'm going to call on him soon. Tonight, perhaps."

"Dad is hardly well enough to have visitors yet."

Gary nodded his understanding. "I would be awfully pleased to have your father associated with me when he is well," he said gravely. "Sylvester Boyce has a splendid business brain, and we must not allow it to go to waste."

His words made the future seem very bright for the Boyces, and Sally expressed her gratitude.

Driving back to Ulmer's, she stopped the car three times, drew Gary's check from her purse and stared at it with tear-dimmed eyes. It still seemed too good to be true. But not even the check could drive certain troublesome thoughts from her mind. She had met Gary Neylands many times in the past, at parties and dances, but had felt only a mild interest in him.

She was smiling cheerfully as she entered the display room at Ulmer's. She was picturing Philip Ulmer's surprise and pleasure when he learned that his newest salesman had made good. She saw Jeff Rainey talking to a middle-aged couple, who were plainly people of moderate circumstances.

Jeff's voice floated to her, bringing her to a halt, gasping. "Tell you a secret," Jeff was saying to them. "The Ford car is every bit as good as the Duluth."

The man and woman smiled pleasedly. "We're sorry we bothered you, Mister," the man said. "We thought the Duluth was a low-priced car."

"Glad you came in," Jeff said heartily. "You buy yourselves a Ford and you'll never regret it."

Sally watched the couple leave, then turned amazed eyes to Jeff. "And you call yourself a salesman!" she whispered.

"I am," Jeff allowed, grinning. "And a good one."

"Then why did you tell them a Ford is as good as a Duluth?" she asked indignantly.

"Because they have enough money for a Ford, but not enough for a Duluth," Jeff explained. "I wanted to send them away happy."

"And so you knocked the Duluth!" Sally sniffed.

Jeff grinned at her. "I've sold two Duluths today, Miss Spitfire. How many did you sell?"

"You sold two cars?" she said resentfully.

Jeff nodded. "Best day I've had in months. But you haven't answered my question."

"I sold one," Sally said proudly, "and I believe that I will sell many more."

"Philip Ulmer doesn't pay commissions on beliefs," Jeff laughed. Then he eyed her narrowly. "Did you really sell a car?"

Sally didn't hate anybody—not even Jeff Rainey—as she took that beautiful check from her bag and handed it to him. When Jeff's eyes rose from the check, they held both surprise and admiration. He grinned at her. "Remind me to kiss you again, Sally . . . sometime when I'm not busy." Then he bowed formally. "Ulmer Motor Sales Company is proud of its new salesman."

CHAPTER 6

Angry Eyes

Sally thought that she could be angry with Jeff, but it was impossible at the moment. He was impudence personified, but, with Gary Neylands' check in her purse, she felt very kindly toward the whole world. And Jeff had said that Ulmer Motor Sales Company was proud of her. These were heartwarming words, even when she considered the source of them.

Jeff grinned at her. "Feeling pretty proud of yourself, Sally?"

"We needed the money so badly," Sally replied. Then she asked, "How much commission do I get?" When he told her, she gasped.

"But you can't hope to sell a car every day," Jeff cautioned her. "Good luck, like bad, comes in big chunks."

She asked, "Are you going to Gary Neylands' party Saturday night?"

"I suppose so," Jeff said indifferently. "For lack of something better to do."

Sally found his manner irritating. "Gary Neylands is a very influential man," she reminded him. "And I happen to know that he is interested in you."

"In me?" Jeff asked, smiling a little.

"In your ideas," Sally amended. "Gary said today that he would like to have his experts work on some of your ideas."

"Gary should employ experts who have ideas of their own," Jeff said dryly.

"But how do you expect to make money out of them, unless they are put on the market?"

"I want to be sure that I will make money out of them," Jeff evaded.

"Don't you trust Gary Neylands?" she asked.

"I don't," Jeff admitted bluntly. "But don't misunderstand; Gary is a cleaver businessman. It's just that I don't want to do business with him myself."

"That sounds unreasonable," Sally charged, and studied his face carefully. "Perhaps you think my father will help you. If you do, you will be disappointed because he couldn't help you even if he wanted to."

Jeff smiled at her. "I'm afraid you don't know your father very well."

Sally colored. Was Jeff another of those who believed that her father had money hidden away?

"Dad hasn't a cent," she said angrily.

"I know that," Jeff said quietly. "I didn't mean what you seem to think."

Sally realized that he was telling the truth, and her anger gave way to puzzlement. "Gary wants my father to work for him when he is well."

"Just a bighearted guy," Jeff jeered.

"You're one of those suspicious people," Sally accused, and was displeased to remember that she too had felt suspicious of Gary Neylands.

"How was your father this morning?" Jeff inquired.

"He seemed better," Sally replied without stopping to think. The sudden twinkle in Jeff's eyes made her add hastily, "But not much better."

"You should fire Dr. Frobisher and put me in charge of the case," Jeff declared.

Sally turned on her heels and made for Philip Ulmer's office. She wanted to see her employer's eyes widen when she told him about her sale to Gary Neylands. And she very definitely had no time to waste on an irritating person like Jeff Rainey.

~ ~ ~

When Sally arrived home that night, she noticed that her mother looked worried. Sally told her about her sale of a Duluth, but even her mother's gloomy expression did not change. After supper Sally pressed her for an explanation.

"I hate to tell you, Sally. You have enough to worry about."

"But you must tell me," Sally persisted, frightened by the tears in her mother's eyes.

"It's your father, Sally. Dr. Frobisher examined him again today and he's worried about his condition."

Sally's fear made it hard for her to speak. "What— what did Dr. Frobisher say?"

"He said that we should take Sylvester to a specialist in New York, and then take him south for the winter." Mrs. Boyce gave a little moan. "I don't know what we are going to do."

Sally thought of the commission she had made today and it seemed very insignificant in the face of what she had just heard. It would take hundreds, perhaps thousands, of dollars to follow the doctor's advice. But she put an arm about her mother and managed to speak calmly. "Don't worry, dear. We'll manage it somehow."

"But we have no money," Mrs. Boyce sobbed.

Sally held her mother very tight. "I'll get the money," she promised. "Dad is going to get what he needs." And her thoughts carried it still further, "No matter what I have to do to get it."

The telephone in the hall was ringing and Sally went to answer it. She had a date with Walter tonight, to go to a movie, and she supposed he was calling to say that he would be late. He often was, now that he was selling insurance. But she learned that it was even more disappointing than that.

"I'll have to break our date darling," Water told her. "I have a prospect for a big policy, but I must see him tonight."

"This must be our lucky day, Walter." And then she told him about the sale she had made.

"Gary Neylands is a fine person," Walter said earnestly. "We must be friendly to him. If he gives me that job, it means that we can be married."

Sally's thoughts rebelled at Walter's plans for marriage because their fortunes rested so firmly in Gary's hands. "Who are you going to see tonight?" she asked, and was conscious of his brief pause.

"Richard Ives."

That was Louise Ives' father, and Sally remembered the girl's declaration that she intended to marry Walter.

"He's too busy to see me during the day," Walter explained. "So he asked me to come to his house tonight."

"Tell Louise hello for me," Sally said lightly, and wondered if her voice had expressed more than she intended.

"Jealous, darling?" Walter laughed.

"Of course not," Sally said sharply, and had an uneasy suspicion that she was. A little bit, anyway.

"This is strictly a business call," Walter told her. "I don't imagine that Louise will be there."

Sally imagined something quite different, but she didn't put it into words.

"I'll see you tomorrow night sure," Walter said.

Sally went slowly up the stairs, dreading to see her father. "To New York to see a specialist; south for the winter." The words were a doleful refrain running through her mind. Her thoughts moved frantically as she searched for a means to bring this about. Sally composed her face, opened the door and entered the room.

"Hello, dear!"

She came to a halt, staring at him in amazement. Mr. Boyce was sitting up in bed, a business review on his knees. There was color in his cheeks, a faint sparkle in his eyes. Sally moved quickly to the bedside. His shining eyes and the color in his face could mean but one thing—fever! She put a trembling hand of his forehead and found that it was cool. "How do you feel, Dad?" she asked uneasily.

"Better than in a long time," Mr. Boyce replied, smiling.

"I think you should lie down," she said, still anxious because of his flushed face. Her eyes went to the business review he had been reading. "You must not think about business until you are a lot better."

"Nonsense!" Mr. Boyce retorted. "It will do me good to think about business. Jeff Rainey said so."

Sally compressed her lips. "You must not see Jeff again. Dr. Frobisher has said that you shouldn't have visitors."

Sylvester Boyce chuckled. "Jeff says that doctors don't know everything."

Sally frowned at him reprovingly. "A man like Jeff can't possibly be good for you Dad."

"I don't agree with you," Mr. Boyce said quietly. "Jeff is so full of vitality that . . . well, he makes me feel stronger and better in every way."

"I told him he must not come here again—" Sally began, and broke off as she heard an authoritative knock at the front door. She glanced suspiciously at her father, saw the twinkle in his eyes.

"So you ordered Jeff not to come here again?" he teased.

Sally frowned at him, hearing voices downstairs—one, her mother's protesting, the other, masculine and genial and determined. Her mother's voice died and footsteps were mounting the stairs, apparently three steps at a time. Those same footsteps were pounding along the hallway. Sally's angry eyes went to the door, just as it burst open.

"Hello, Jeff!" Sylvester Boyce said happily. "You arrived just in time to rescue me from Sally."

Jeff ignored Sally's scowl, greeting them cheerfully. "If Sally tries to boss you," he threatened, grinning, "just send for me."

"I'll remember that," Mr. Boyce smiled.

"Sally is a rather pretty girl," Jeff said judicially, "when she's mad."

"We think she's pretty all the time," Mr. Boyce laughed.

"I don't know that I can agree with you," Jeff said doubtfully.

CHAPTER 7

Too Good to be True

Sally's feelings of irritation vanished before Gary Neylands' friendly, admiring gaze. He looked so well groomed, so competent—so everything that Jeff Rainey was not. She introduced him to her mother, and saw her mother's face light up with interest.

"It was good of you to buy a car from Sally," Mrs. Boyce murmured gratefully.

Gary shook his head, smiling. "I needed a car, Mrs. Boyce. I won't have Sally feeling under obligations to me."

Sally felt comforted by his words as they moved into the living room. She had felt under obligations to him and hadn't liked the feeling.

Gary smiled at her again as they seated themselves. "Are you wondering why I called here tonight?"

Sally was wondering, but she denied it. "I was preparing to spend a lonely evening. Walter was to take me to a movie, but he had to see a prospect about an insurance policy."

"That's too bad," Gary sympathized. "I mean, about the movie. I'm delighted to hear that Walter is doing better."

"Sally tells me that you are trying to find a place for Walter in your business," Mrs. Boyce said. "I do hope that you can."

Sally saw that her mother was pleased to have a successful man like Gary here. During the past years, Mrs. Boyce had entertained most of the leading men of the state, and Sally knew that she missed these affairs.

"I'm going to do everything I can for Walter," Gary promised; then he looked at Sally again. "I saw Samuel Spring at my club tonight, Sally. I believe that you can sell him a Duluth."

"Do you really mean it?" Sally gasped.

"He was thinking of buying another car," Gary smiled. "But I told him how please I was with the Duluth, and he wants you to call on him."

Sally's heart was a feather, fluttering about within her breast. If she could just sell enough cars. But she faced the truth, with a sinking heart. She couldn't possibly sell enough Duluths to send her father to that specialist.

"I appreciate your kindness," she said simply, and Gary's expression said that he was amply repaid for his trouble.

Gary turned to Mrs. Boyce, "How is your husband?"

Mrs. Boyce shook her head sadly. "He isn't doing at all well, Mr. Neylands. Dr. Frobisher says that we should take him to a specialist in New York, then south for the winter."

Gary's eyes expressed the proper sympathy. "Dr. Frobisher is an excellent physician. You should follow his advice, by all means."

Mrs. Boyce's thin shoulders sank. "If we only could . . . but it is impossible."

Gary gave her a grave smile. "Has Sally told you that I am making plans for Mr. Boyce's future?"

Mrs. Boyce glanced inquiringly at Sally, then at Gary again. "Sally didn't tell me."

"You may think it presumptuous of me," he said suavely, "but I want Mr. Boyce in my business when he recovers."

Seeing her mother's entranced eyes, it seemed to Sally that she could read her thoughts: "This is the proper husband for Sally; he is young, handsome, successful!"

"You are very kind, Mr. Neylands," Mrs. Boyce said in a tearful voice. "We do need friends so badly."

"Is Mr. Boyce well enough to leave for the east?" Gary asked quietly.

Sally looked at her mother, and saw her own puzzlement in her mother's face.

"I— I hardly know," Mrs. Boyce said uncertainly.

"I'm going to put my card on the table," Gary told them. "I need Mr. Boyce in my business, and so I want him to get well as quickly as possible."

"I'm afraid I don't understand," Mrs. Boyce said.

"I would like to finance his trip east, so that he can come to my plant in the spring," Gary replied.

"But we couldn't accept money from you," Mrs. Boyce said weakly.

"I understand how you feel," Gary said smoothly. "But you don't understand how I feel. I'm a businessman, Mrs. Boyce. I invest in brains, just as I invest in stocks and bonds. And brains, I might say, are the best investment of all."

"But Sylvester isn't fit for business," Mrs. Boyce protested. "We aren't sure that he will ever get well."

"I called on Dr, Frobisher this afternoon," Gary said. "He tells me that your husband will get well if he receives the proper treatment."

Sally's thoughts were crying a question suddenly, "What does Gary expect in return for all this? What does he want?" And she remembered, guiltily, that she had dubbed Jeff Rainey a suspicious person.

"I— I don't know what to say," Mrs. Boyce sighed.

"Please don't think that I'm posing as a philanthropist," Gary Neylands laughed. "When I spend money, I expect to get an adequate return." He was grave again.

"I really consider Mr. Boyce a splendid investment. As he is now, he isn't valuable to me, or to you, his family. A few thousand dollars will get him well, and then he will be of value to both of us."

"I don't know what Sylvester will think," Mrs. Boyce told him. "But I am grateful for your offer. You can talk to my husband when he is well enough to see visitors."

Sally heard footsteps in the upstairs hallway, and remembered that Jeff was still with her father. Gary looked at her inquiringly, but Sally only shrugged.

"It's Jeff Rainey," Mrs. Boyce explained to Gary. "He insisted on seeing my husband tonight. It's almost impossible to keep him out of the house."

Sally saw that Gary was not pleased and hastened to make an additional explanation. "We've told him Dad isn't well enough to see visitors, but he just bursts into the house anyway." Sally broke off, flushing. It sounded rather silly to admit that you couldn't keep an undesired visitor out of the house; and she realized that Gary was puzzled. Footsteps were pounding down the stairs, and, a moment later, Jeff Rainey charged into the room.

"The service here is terrible," Jeff complained, then came to a stop as he saw Gary Neylands. "Hi, Gary! How's the auto gadget business?"

Gary Neylands got to his feet, a rather forced smile on his lips. "I am doing very well," he said coolly."

Jeff gave a jerky little bow. "You have to excuse me. I'm headed for the icebox." Jeff was gone for a few minutes, then he bustled through the room again, a pitcher of cracked ice in one hand, two glasses balanced precariously in the other. He grinned at Sally as he passed her. "Don't run away, little girl," he ordered. "I may find time to take you riding after awhile."

Sally sank back in her chair, gasping, feeling that a hurricane had just swept through the room.

"A very tempestuous person," Gary Neylands said, and his voice was edged with irritation.

"Very!" Mrs. Boyce agreed heartily.

"Jeff is hardly the person I would choose to visit me if I were ill," Gary said with a wry smile. "But Jeff isn't quite as bad as he sounds. He's rather a brainy fellow, and I hope to market some of the auto accessories he has invented."

Mrs. Boyce's eyes were very wide. "Do you mean to say that Jeff Rainey has invented something of importance?"

"Strange as it may seem, he has; and I intend to fill his pockets with money, if he will let me." Gary smiled faintly. "And make some money for myself, of course."

Sally felt her suspicions flame up afresh. Gary Neylands was just too good to be true. He spoke well of everybody; he had beneficent plans for everybody; but she could not kill her suspicion that he was thinking always of Gary Neylands. She bit her lip in exasperation. Gary had admitted frankly why he wanted to help her father and Jeff Rainey. He admitted quite frankly that he was no philanthropist.

Gary rose to his feet, smiling down at Mrs. Boyce. "Perhaps I will be allowed to see your husband soon, Mrs. Boyce?" He looked at Sally, and his smile said that the three of them were allies. "We must do our best to get Mr. Boyce to listen to reason. There is no reason why he should remain sick, when he can so easily get well."

"I'll speak to Sylvester," Mrs. Boyce promised.

But Gary was staring down at Sally now, and she was reminded of the promise she had made her mother earlier in the evening, that she would get the money needed to send Sylvester Boyce to that New York specialist. Then Gary Neylands had appeared at the front door and had made the impossible possible. No struggle or self-denial was necessary, no waiting, no worrying, no painstaking saving of pennies. All that she had to do was to agree to permit him to work the miracle. And he had told them what he wanted in return—only the brains of Sylvester Boyce when he should become well.

"I— I don't know what to say," Sally faltered, and was angry because she hadn't agreed to do what he wanted.

Gary stared at her for a moment longer, his eyes warming. "Then we won't speak of it any more tonight," he said easily, and turned to the door. He stopped, glanced at Sally. "Did you say that Walter was unable to take you to a movie tonight?"

Sally stared at him curiously. "Yes, but it isn't important."

"I have the evening free," Gary said suavely. "Could I take Walter's place for one evening?"

Sally hesitated, looking at her mother. Mrs. Boyce nodded vigorously, smiling.

"Run along to a movie, dear," her mother urged her. "There's no reason why you shouldn't go."

But Sally was thinking of Jeff's impudent order: "Don't run away, little girl. I may find time to take you riding." Frowning, she rose to her feet. "Thanks, Gary. I'd like to go with you."

CHAPTER 8

Expectations?

Leaving the theater with Gary Neylands, two hours later, Sally found that she didn't recall much of the picture. Troubled thoughts had come between her and the figures moving across the screen. Most troublesome of all was her feeling that Gary was assuming a too important place in her affairs. He made it all appear innocuous, made her suspicions seem contemptible, but she could not banish them. She could not shut her eyes to the fact Walter's future, her father's, her own, were being shaped by Gary Neylands.

"Shall we drop by my apartment?" Gary suggested as they were entering the car.

Sally's suspicions burned brighter. His bachelor apartment was located on top of Avondale's tallest business building.

"I'm going to have it redecorated soon," he continued suavely; "and I'd like to have your opinion."

Sally felt confused. Everything Gary did and said showed his liking for her. But was it mere friendliness—hoping for no reward—or was it a prelude to something else?

Her lips tightened suddenly. If Gary expected more than she had to give, she might as well know it now. And so she nodded her agreement.

"I hear that girls find Jeff quite irresistible," Gary laughed.

Sally was remembering the adoring face of that ravishing blond who had bought a car from Jeff. She sniffed. "I find it hard to understand," she said coldly.

"I'm told that Carol Putnam is badly smitten with him," Gary continued. "But like you, I find it hard to understand."

Sally felt bewildered. She had known Carol Putnam all her life, and while they were not intimate friends, she had respect for Carol's intelligence. Carol's father had died recently, leaving her one of the richest girls in the state.

Ten minutes later they reached Gary's apartment and a Filipino boy admitted them. Gary dismissed him and led Sally through a short hall to the living room. A thick Turkestan rug, almost blood red, was spread over the floor and modernistic furniture was scattered about. Sally became increasingly uneasy as she followed him through the apartment. Each room was beautifully decorated and furnished and everything looked quite new. Gary led her finally through French doors to a terrace and the lights of Avondale twinkled below them.

They seated themselves and Gary smiled at her. "What do you think of my little place, Sally?"

"It's very lovely," Sally replied. "I don't see why you should want to change it."

"Very lovely, perhaps," Gary said soberly, "but it is very lonely at times." He looked away from her, and there was a note of sadness in his voice. "When I was a lad, I dreamed of something like this. I didn't know that it could be so empty."

Sally wondered how many girls had occupied this terrace with him and heard the same words. "You will get married someday," she said lightly, "and then it won't seem so lonely." Gary looked at her and something in his eyes set her heart pounding.

"It isn't quite so simple as that, Sally. I had almost given up hopes of finding the right girl."

Sally sighed her relief as he looked away from her. Had he interested himself in Walter as a means of earning her liking and gratitude, hoping that she would learn to like Walter less and Gary Neylands more? Gary was silent, but it seemed to Sally that she knew the declaration forming in his mind. He would turn to her in a moment, declare his passion for her, attempt to take her in his arms. And she, tied to Walter by the bonds of love, must refuse to listen, must tell him frankly that she could never learn to care for him. But this, she realized miserably, would bring to an end Walter's chance of a decent job, would bring to an end her chance of sending her father to that specialist!

Gary Neylands rose to his feet, smiled down at her. "I know that you are anxious about your father, so I will take you home now." He smiled ruefully. "However, I won't pretend to enjoy seeing you leave."

Sally was filled with amazement and the feeling quickly gave way to one of shame. While she had been nursing those hateful suspicions, Gary had been worrying about her father. Following him indoors, she vowed that never again would she distrust Gary Neylands. Never!

The telephone was jangling as they entered the living room, and Sally watched the Filipino boy answer it. "Yes. Mr. Neylands is here."

"Wait!" Gary said irritably, but he was too late, for the boy was replacing the receiver. Gary scowled at him. "Who is it?"

"Mr. Norris has come to keep his appointment," the boy replied.

"I had no appointment for tonight," Gary snapped.

Sally was watching the boy's face and saw him grow pale under Gary's furious glance.

"I made a mistake," the boy's voice trembled.

Gary turned to Sally as the boy shuffled from the room. He smiled apologetically. "Walter is coming up to the apartment, Sally. Would you care to . . . disappear?"

"Disappear?" Sally repeated, puzzled. "But why should I?"

Gary's eye moved over her face, then he shrugged. "I was afraid Walter might not understand," he said easily.

"I have no secrets from Walter," Sally said quietly. "You see, we love and trust each other." Meeting his steady gaze, Sally thought that she had never known anyone whose emotions were under such perfect control.

"How very nice," Gary said tonelessly.

A buzzer sounded and the Filipino boy went to answer it. He reappeared in a moment, with Walter Norris beside him.

"Hello, Gary! Am I late?" Walter said, and then his eyes swung to Sally and his smile vanished. "Sally! You here?" he whispered.

Sally greeted him cheerfully and tried not to see the suspicion and resentment, which showed in his eyes.

"Have a seat, Walter," Gary said genially.

"What are you doing here, Sally?" Walter asked bluntly.

Sally sank down on a sofa, and Walter seated himself beside her, his narrowed eyes on her face.

"I wanted to see this lovely apartment," Sally replied.

"I'm thinking of redecorating it," Gary broke in. "I wanted Sally's opinion."

Sally's troubled eyes went to Gary. Had he wanted Walter to find her here alone with him, hoping that Walter would misunderstand? She sighed as she remembered her vow, of five minutes ago, that she would never distrust Gary again.

"I came by your house," Walter told her. "I wanted to tell you that I sold Mr. Ives a big insurance policy."

"Did Mother tell you that I had gone to a movie with Gary?"

Walter nodded, frowning. "Yes. She told me."

"I'm so glad you sold a policy," Sally said, then she asked mischievously, "Was Louise at home?"

Walter looked at her quickly, then away again. "Yes. Louise was at home. But I spent the evening talking to her father."

Gary Neylands sank into a nearby chair, glanced at Walter. "I forgot that you had an appointment with me tonight, Walter." He shook his head. "I haven't anything definite to tell you, yet. You might come to my office sometime next week."

Sally saw resentment in Walter's face and found herself sharing it. She looked at Gary appealingly. "I do hope you can find work for Walter soon. He doesn't like the insurance business."

Gary smiled faintly. "Do you like to sell, Sally?"

I rather enjoy it," Sally admitted, laughing. "It's just like a game."

"I hate it!" Walter growled. "You have to be so damned pleasant to people you despise."

Sally put her hand on Walter's, pitying him. He had been such a good-natured boy when he worked for her father at the bank. She felt that he would be that again when he found more congenial work.

"Don't you think we should tell Walter what we are planning for your father, Sally," Gary asked suddenly.

He seemed to take her astonished silence for consent and repeated to Walter what he had told her and her mother. Sally glanced at Walter and saw puzzlement and resentment in his face, and knew that he hated it because Gary was able to do what he, Walter, could not do.

"But what if Mr. Boyce doesn't get well?" Walter asked when Gary had finished. "You'll be out your money, with no chance of getting it back."

"Dr. Frobisher says that he will get well," Gary replied rather coldly. "I'm content to take his word for it." His eyes went to Sally. "I don't believe I would tell your father where the money is coming from, Sally. Sick people are inclined to be unreasonable."

Sally shook her head; she couldn't agree to this. "Dad might not want to enter your business, Gary. We can't accept your loan until Dad agrees to do that."

"That sounds reasonable," Walter commented.

Gary gave him a cold look. "Is there any reason they shouldn't accept a loan from me?"

Sally saw color steal into Walter's cheeks and braced herself for an angry outburst. But he merely said mildly, "No, Gary. I know of no reason."

CHAPTER 9

Million Dollar Idea

Listening to Gary's offer of a loan, which would make it possible to send her father to a New York specialist, Sally had a queer feeling that she was in the palm of a giant hand, with the powerful fingers relentlessly closing in on her. And that, rack her brain as she might, there was no escape. "I don't know," she whispered, and saw Gary's eyes harden as they went to Walter Norris. Sally got quickly to her feet, finding it difficult to breathe. "I think I had better go home. I can't decide anything tonight. After all, it's really for Mother to decide."

"Would you mind taking Sally home, Walter? I have a little work to do before I turn in."

That commanding voice brought fresh color to Walter's face; but he only said, "Of course. Glad to."

Gary went with them to the door. "Don't forget to see Samuel Spring tomorrow, Sally. I believe I've sold him on the Duluth, but you mustn't let him slip through your fingers."

"I'll telephone him the first thing in the morning," Sally promised.

"Then, goodnight," Gary said softly, "and thank you for a very delightful evening."

~ ~ ~

Riding across town—to the less desirable side of town—Sally stared straight ahead, but she was conscious of Walter slouched behind the wheel, of his brooding silence. He hadn't spoken a word since leaving Gary's apartment, but his very silence told her that he shared her resentment at the way events were shaping themselves. Or, rather, at the way Gary Neylands was shaping them.

"I wonder if Gary is stalling me about that job," Walter growled presently. "He keeps putting me off from day to day, until I don't know what to think."

"If Gary doesn't give you a job," Sally said comfortingly, "then you will find one with some other company."

Walter's sigh was almost a groan. "I hate selling, Sally. It's too much like asking favors of people, and I've always hated to ask favors."

"I can't see why you should feel that way," Sally protested. "I don't feel that people are doing me a favor when they buy a Duluth. I believe that the Duluth is worth what they pay for it."

"I'm glad you enjoy it!" Walter said almost savagely. "But I don't, and I never will. I'm damned sick of having doors slammed in my face."

Sally leaned her head against his shoulder, pitying him, wanting to comfort him, but knowing that no words of hers could change his attitude. He had been raised as a rich woman's son and was not able to face the hard realities of the modern business world. And she was beginning to doubt that he would be any happier in another business. She sat up straight, her lips firm. This was not time for her to be weak. "I'm sure that something better is in store for us," she said stoutly. "I believe that you will find work that you like, and that we can be married soon. We must be patient—"

"Patient!" Walter growled. "I've run out of patience. I'm beginning to believe that nothing will ever be right again."

Sally held her voice steady by an effort. "You must not feel that way, Walter."

"No doubt you'll fail me next," he said sullenly. "It didn't make me feel very good to find you at Gary's apartment."

Sally choked down the bitter retort that shaped itself in her thoughts. "You are not yourself tonight, Walter."

"I'm myself, all right," he said crossly. "I don't want you to go to his apartment again."

Sally sank back in her seat, her eyes dimmed with tears. "You must not give me orders, Walter. We are modern people. We respect and love each other."

Walter gave her an angry demanding glance. "Promise me that you won't go there again, Sally."

Sally shook her head. "I have no intention of going there again, but I can't promise not to. If I did, it would mean that I felt guilty, and I don't."

Walter was angrily silent until they reached her house; and he didn't appear to notice Jeff Rainey's car, parked just ahead. He leaned across Sally, opened the door.

"Good night," he said crossly.

Sally turned to him, her eyes pleading. "Don't act that way, Walter. We have enough troubles, goodness knows, without inventing any. We must not let anything kill the love we have for each other."

Walter's face looked a little less grim. "I don't like the idea of your accepting money from Gary," he said huskily. "It just doesn't look right, Sally."

"But you told Gary that it was a good idea," Sally reminded him.

"That's right; blame it all on me," he complained.

Sally slipped quickly through the open door. She felt that they were headed inexorably toward a quarrel, and she didn't want that. They had nothing left but their love for each other. If they lost that, life would be empty for both of them. "Don't forget that we are going to Gary's country place tomorrow night," she said softly.

There was shame in the eyes he turned to her. "I'm a brute, darling," he said gloomily. "Will you forgive me?"

Sally leaned forward and kissed him; her throat was too full of tears for words. This boy she loved was really decent and kind and, in all ways, worthy of her love.

Entering the house, Sally found that her mother had retired; but a mutter of voices told her that Jeff Rainey and her father were still talking. Going swiftly up the stairs, she glanced at her wristwatch and frowned when she saw that it was past midnight. Lips tight, she went to the door of her father's bedroom.

". . . it's a million-dollar idea, if I ever heard one," Sylvester Boyce was saying enthusiastically. Then he saw Sally. "Hello, darling."

Jeff Rainey looked up, grinned. "Hello, darling!" he echoed, surveying her with guileless blue eyes.

Sally very pointedly ignored Jeff. She choked down the anger his "Hello, darling" had aroused in her and glanced reprovingly at her father. "It's after midnight," she said sternly.

"Is it?" Sylvester Boyce said without interest, and turned to Jeff again. "It's strange that no one thought of that idea before."

“It’s the obvious things they overlook,” Jeff replied. “I honestly believe that we can make some money out of it.”

Sylvester Boyce looked at Sally again. “Jeff has an idea for a radiator and gas tank cap. It makes it unnecessary for the filling-station attendant to remove the caps when he is filling your car with water and gasoline.” He glanced at Jeff. “Tell Sally about it.”

Jeff tried unsuccessfully to look modest. “It’s only a million-dollar idea,” he deprecated. “Hardly worth mentioning.”

“Then don’t mention it!” Sally snapped.

“I suppose I’ll have to explain it, since you insist,” Jeff said blandly, and proceeded to do so, ignoring her angry eyes.

Jeff’s voice was crisply businesslike as he drew a word picture of the device; and Sally’s anger gave way to bewilderment and then, slowly and unwillingly, to admiration. He was describing a radiator and gas tank cap with a spring top, which, during the filling operation, would be depressed by the nozzles of the water and gas hoses. The cap would spring shut when the nozzles were lifted. Listening raptly to Jeff, Sally remembered how much time the station attendants consumed in removing the two caps. This device of Jeff’s would, she saw clearly, cut the filling time in half.

Jeff’s eyes twinkled at her when he had finished. “Well, what’s the verdict, Miss Spitfire?”

Sally swallowed the words of praise that trembled on her lips. Never, never would Jeff Rainey get an encouraging word out of her. She glanced at her father and noticed for the first time the sparkle in his eyes. He was looking so much better.

Jeff got to his feet, stretched, yawned contentedly. “Guess I’d better run along, Mr. Boyce. See you again soon.”

There was a purposeful gleam in Sally’s eyes as she followed him to the door and on down the stairs. He was expecting her father to help him with his inventions; and he might as well be told that Sylvester Boyce was going to do nothing of the kind. Jeff grabbed his hat from the hall rack, opened the front door.

“Wait, Jeff!”

Jeff wheeled about, his eyebrows raised. “Anything wrong?”

“You mustn’t come here again,” Sally said coldly. “My father isn’t going to help market your ideas. When he gets well, he is going into Gary Neylands’ business.”

Jeff looked amiable but doubtful. "Does your father know about this, Sally?"

"It doesn't concern you," she said stiffly. "I just don't want you to come here again."

Silently, Jeff turned and went through the door, closing it softly behind him. Sally stared at the door, amazed at her own anger, but more amazed that Jeff should have left so peacefully. She stood there, hearing his footsteps, hearing his car door slam shut. She heard the whine of his starter but the engine remained silent. The starter whined, again and again, and when Sally felt that she could stand that nerve-wracking sound no longer, she opened the door. He might want her to telephone for a wrecker.

When Sally reached the roadster, she thrust her head inside. "What seems to be the matter—"

Jeff's lips met her with fury.

She jerked back, gasping. "You— you tricked me!" she wailed. Jeff stepped on the starter and the motor roared. He looked mildly ashamed of himself. "I hated to leave without kissing you good night, Sally," he said soberly.

CHAPTER 10

Her Malicious Smile

Saturday night, and dinner was being served in the spacious dining room at Gary Neylands' country home. Sally was feeling unpleasantly conspicuous. She could not understand even now, while deft waiters removed the consomm□ plates, why Gary had placed her in the hostess' seat facing him. He had brought Louise Ives tonight, but Louise was seated at Sally's left. At Sally's right—but she preferred not even to glance in that direction—there was sandy hair there, mocking blue eyes, a derisive smile: Jeff Rainey, hateful person, who lured girls out of houses and kissed them against their will. Sally's eyes went blankly past Jeff and touched Walter Norris and Carol Putnam, who were seated across from each other farther down the table. She had known Carol all her life but was amazed now, as always, that so much sheer beauty could be found in one girl. Carol was dressed simply in white, but it was a perfect foil for her flaxen hair, her violet eyes and milky skin. Sally's brows knit in a puzzled frown. How could a girl so beautiful and intelligent love an impudent, blundering person like Jeff Rainey?

"Have you forgotten what I told you at the country club?" Louise Ives asked softly.

Sally thought fretfully that Gary might have been more considerate than to place her between Louise and Jeff. She looked at Louise, widening her eyes. "I'm afraid I have Louise. Was it something important?"

Louise's red lips curved in a malicious smile. "I don't think you've forgotten, Sally. I want you to know that I haven't changed my mind. I'm going to marry Walter.

Sally shrugged and her eyes wandered down the table to Walter. His gloomy eyes were fixed on the squab on his plate; he seemed sunk in troubled thought. Gary Neylands was chatting with Carol Putnam, but his eyes came to meet Sally's and said that he was pleased to have her seated at his table. Sally looked quickly away from him. She was experiencing again tonight that queer feeling that she was held in the palm of a giant hand, whose steel fingers were closing in on her.

"How is your father feeling today, Sally?"

Sally made her face cold as she looked at Jeff Rainey. He had not been to the house since the night he tricked her out of the house and kissed her. Sylvester Boyce had seemed much better that night, she remembered; and he had sat up for an hour the next day, for the first time since he had become ill. But now, with three days gone, he had relapsed into his old condition.

"He doesn't appear to be any better," she replied, and thought resentfully that Jeff was almost handsome in his dinner jacket. At least he looked rugged and manly and sure of himself. She felt uneasy under his steady, grave regard.

'Won't you allow me to call on him again?" Jeff asked quietly. "I honestly believe that my visits were good for him." There was a very faint twinkle in his eyes. "If you let me visit him, I'll promise to behave myself, Sally."

But his words reminded her of his outrageous conduct, and the memory made her voice shake. "You are not to come to my house again," she said, and colored, knowing that she had spoken too loudly.

"You can come to my house whenever you like, Jeff," Louise Ives offered, laughing.

Jeff cocked a bland eye at Louise. "I'll make a note of that, Louise." He turned to Sally again. "What is Dr. Frobisher's diagnosis of your father's troubles?"

Sally's eyes went to him, unwilling. She was puzzled by this new and more serious Jeff Rainey. "Dr. Frobisher calls it a nervous breakdown. He can't find anything else wrong with him, but I feel sure that there is."

"Has it occurred to you that his trouble might be entirely psychological, Sally?"

"I'm not a doctor," Sally said stiffly, "and so I can't discuss it."

"Your father looked much better than the last time I saw him," Jeff said quietly, his eyes searching her face. Then he asked, "Would you let your feeling for me stand in the way of his recovery, Sally?"

The question stung and she bit her lip. She couldn't deny that Sylvester Boyce had seemed a lot better; and she could think of no other reason for this improvement except Jeff's visits. "I prefer not to talk about it," she said uneasily. "I'm sure that your visits did not help him."

"I have a real fondness for your father," Jeff told her. "I wouldn't do anything to hurt him, and I believe that my visits help him."

Sally found herself close to agreeing with him, but she couldn't admit it. He had been so impudent, so hateful.

"I was giving your father something more important to him than medicine," Jeff said gravely.

Sally met his eyes squarely, not wanting to ask the question, but finding it impossible not to. "What is this important something you were giving my father?" she asked.

"Hope."

Sally's thoughts repeated the word, and her heart beat faster. Yes, that was what she had seen in her father's eyes after Jeff's visits. During those visits, Sylvester Boyce found it possible to climb out of the pit of hopelessness and to find hope again. A wave of shame swept over her suddenly. Jeff had helped her father, had wanted to help him more, but she had allowed her silly feelings to stand in the way. Well, she would tell Jeff that she had been wrong. She looked at Jeff but he was chatting with Carol Putnam now and the girl's face was tinged with color, her eyes were alive and eager.

Louise Ives' husky whisper cut into Sally's meditations.

"Don't you think you had better turn Walter loose, before he turns you lose, Sally?"

Sally looked at the girl, hardly comprehending. "I'm afraid I don't understand you, Louise. And certainly you don't understand me and Walter."

Louise's red lips were twisted. "You mean, you don't want to understand," she whispered furiously.

Sally found that she couldn't share Louise's anger. You couldn't be angry with anyone who was so appallingly outspoken. Sally smiled a little. "You are being childish, Louise. You want Walter only because you can't have him."

Louise's smile was bitter. "If that were only true," she sighed. "But it isn't true. I'll always love him."

Listening to that steady, bitter voice, Sally was almost convinced. But it was hard for her to believe that Louise, who had flirted with so many men, could be really sincere about one. "I'm sorry, Louise," Sally said gently.

Louise's dark eyes sparkled resentfully. "You don't love him, Sally," she accused. "If you did, you would free him from his engagement to you. Can't you see that he is losing his grip on himself?"

"No, I can't," Sally retorted, and was angry because her voice sounded unsure.

"You are determined to make a business man out of him, even if it kills him," Louise charged.

Sally's feelings of compassion died before this accusation. "Walter is at liberty to do what he wants to do," she replied stiffly.

Louis's whisper trembled angrily. "Walter feels tied to you. You know as well as I do, that he isn't capable of making up his own mind."

"Walter is going to work for Gary Neylands soon," Sally said coldly.

"Do you really believe that?" Louise jeered.

Sally searched the girl's angry face and remembered her own suspicions. "Of course, I believe it," she said quickly.

Louise leaned toward her; her whisper held the ring of contempt. "You can't be that naive, Sally. You must know that Gary is after you, and that he will throw Walter into the discard when he has served his purpose." Her voice sounded choked suddenly. "I have enough money for both Walter and myself. Won't you free him, Sally?"

Sally forced a smile. "I believe that Gary will give Walter a good position in his business, and I don't believe that Gary has anything but a friendly feeling for me." But she felt uncomfortable before Louise's frankly, contemptuous stare.

Louise's eyes swept the table, returned to Sally. "Gary never does anything without a reason," Louise said firmly. "He expects to make use of every person at this table tonight."

"What an imagination you have," Sally said lightly.

"Gary hopes to persuade Carol to finance an extension to his plant," Louise continued evenly. "He is using Walter as a means of enlisting your sympathy and gratitude. He plans to steal Jeff Rainey's ideas."

"And what does he plan for you?" Sally inquired, smiling.

"He hopes that I will steal Walter from you," Louise said bluntly. "Then it would be easier for him to get you."

Sally's eyes went to Gary. She saw him lean toward Carol Putnam. She couldn't hear what he said, but Carol's reply was audible: "You will have to see Judge Manners, Gary," Carol was saying. "He handles all my investments." Sally looked at Louise and saw that she had heard, too. There was a triumphant gleam in the girl's eyes.

"Gary can't forget his own interests long enough to eat his dinner," Louise purred. Then her voice hardened. "Are you going to turn Walter loose before it is too late?"

"I don't care to talk about it anymore," Sally replied, smiling.

"Then it's war!" Louise said grimly. "And you will lose!"

CHAPTER 11

Resentment

The dinner had ended and Sally was glad. Jeff Rainey had been less irritating than usual, but Louise Ives, seated on her right, had made it impossible for her to enjoy the meal. Dancing with Walter now in the big living room, Sally tried to forget the disturbing things Louise had said. Pat Walter's shoulder, she watched Louise dancing with Gary Neylands. Her glance wandered from them to Jeff Rainey, who was dancing with Carol Putnam. The girl's lovely face was raised to him, and Sally wondered if he returned her love.

"Let's try to get away from here early, Sally," Walter whispered in her ear. "I don't seem to be in a party humor tonight."

"Are you worried about something, Walter?"

"Only the usual things," Walter said gloomily.

Sally found herself sharing his gloom, remembering the debonair Walter of six months ago, realizing how much he had changed.

"I went to see Gary at the plant this afternoon," Walter said sulkily. "He hasn't found an opening for me yet."

Jeff's genial laughter filled the room suddenly, seeming to blend with the music from the radio. Sally cast a resentful glance in his direction. He had no right to be so carefree; he was no better off than Walter. Both had selling jobs, neither had any reserves of money. That booming laughter of Jeff's was like a personal affront to her.

"Jeff gets on my nerves," Walter grumbled. "I don't see how Carol can endure him."

Sally shrugged. Jeff irritated her almost past endurance, but her father respected him and so did Gary Neylands and Carol Putnam. And she, Sally, was beginning to understand that Jeff's twinkling eyes sometimes hid serious, purposeful thoughts.

"I suppose Jeff plans to marry Carol for her money," Walter said cynically.

Sally shook her head. “Carol is beautiful enough to make any man’s heart beat faster.”

“These high-pressure salesmen aren’t capable of feeling human emotions,” Walter growled.

Sally raised reproachful eyes at him. “Have you forgotten that I’m learning to be a salesman?”

“You’ll never be successful at selling,” Walter told her. “You’re too sweet and gentle. When you have sold Duluths to your friends, you’ll be through.”

Sally couldn’t pretend to like this. “The Boyces haven’t enough friends left to make it profitable. I plan to sell Duluths to our bitterest enemies.” But she remembered that, so far, she had sold cars only to Gary and to his friend Samuel Spring. And could only console herself with the thought that she had worked hard every day.

“Has Gary found any more prospects for you?” Walter asked.

Sally looked at him suspiciously, but his eyes evaded hers.

“No, he hasn’t. Why?”

Walter met her eyes suddenly; his smile was bitter. “I don’t know what we’d do without Gary.” His voice was heavy with resentment.

Sally knew that his resentful feeling toward Gary dated from the time he had found her in Gary’s apartment. Walter had said no more about it, but she felt that the memory rankled. “I wish you could find a job with somebody else,” she said quietly.

“Easy to say but hard to do,” he said irritably. “I’ve tried everybody I know.”

“Then why don’t you try somebody you don’t know?” Sally suggested.

“If your friends won’t give you a chance, you can’t expect strangers to. There are too many men out of work.”

“It wouldn’t hurt to try,” Sally persisted.

“I’d only get insulted for my pains. Maybe if you would speak to Gary, he might find a job for me quicker,” Walter said uneasily.

Sally shivered. She didn’t want to ask further favors of Gary. Already she felt weighted down by his kindnesses. Gary hadn’t said anything more about sending her father to that specialist, but she believed that Gary hadn’t forgotten. That he was simply waiting for her and her mother to make their wishes known to him. "I'd rather not ask him, Walter."

"Okay!" he said petulantly. "If you'd rather I went crazy trying to sell insurance, I suppose I'll have to."

Sally kept her temper in check, reminding herself that Walter was not himself now, that he had once been kind and considerate and that he would be again, when he got a job and an assured income. "I'll speak to him, Walter," she said gently. "However, I don't imagine it will do any good."

Walter was silent for a moment, then, "I imagine it will do a great deal of good."

"Let's go powder our shiny noses, Sally."

Sally turned, smiling, to meet Carol Putnam and Jeff Rainey.

Jeff regarded her with critical eyes. "Your nose does need attention, Sally," he grinned. "Walter and I can spare you two for a few minutes."

Sally ignored him and heard Walter's resentful mutter as she walked away with Carol. They came to a stop, staring, as they entered the dressing room. The four walls had been decorated to represent a theater. One wall was painted as a stage, but the actors were monkeys. Sally's bewildered eyes went to the other three walls and found they had been painted to represent the boxes and orchestra pit with every seat filled with monkeys, some in masculine evening dress, others in Parisian frocks and bedecked with jewelry.

"Gary has a very strange sense of humor," Carl Putnam observed dryly.

"It does seem so," Sally agreed fervently, and wondered if the decorations of this room gave a key to Gary Neylands' character.

Did he see himself as a superior being and the rest of the human family as mere monkeys put into the world for his amusement and profit?

Sally found that Carol was looking at her, an amused light in her lovely eyes. She had an uncomfortable feeling that Carol had read her thoughts.

"I have my heart set on a Duluth car," Carol smiled. "But I'm finding it difficult to buy one."

Sally's eyes widened. "But Jeff sells Duluths."

"But not to me," Carol pouted humorously.

"But why?"

"Jeff is a very strange young man," Carol explained, smiling. "He won't sell me a car because he knows that I . . . like him."

That pause was significant; it said that what Carol felt for Jeff was something more profound than mere liking. And that Carol didn't care who knew it.

"Will you sell me a Duluth sometime next week, Sally?"

Sally hesitated for a moment; then she nodded, smiling. "I'll be glad to sell you a car." Her spirits soared as they left that rather horrible dressing room. This was her first sale that had not been engineered by Gary Neylands and it gave her more pleasure.

~ ~ ~

Gary Neylands came to meet them when they entered the living room; and his genial smile included both of them. They chatted for a moment and then Jeff came to claim Carol for a dance.

"I want to speak to you alone, Sally," Gary said as the others moved off.

"Carol is going to buy a car from me," she said happily.

Gary's eyes went blank; his smile looked rather forced. "That's nice," he said too heartily. He led her across the living room and through a door to the dark veranda. Then he turned to her and his smile looked natural again. "I have another prospect lined up for you, Sally. You can meet him and his wife tomorrow morning."

"Tomorrow morning," Sally repeated thoughtfully. "But that's Sunday morning."

"What of it?" Gary shrugged. "I'm playing golf with Fred Swift and his wife at the country club. Fred wants to buy a car, and I asked him to wait until you could show him a Duluth.

Sally looked away from him, troubled. She always spent Sundays with Walter, and she knew he wouldn't like it if she made another engagement. Then she remembered that he had broken a date with her, so that he could sell an insurance policy to Louise Ives' father. "I don't know what to say," she faltered.

"Fred is very busy during the week," Gary persisted. "You might not get another chance to talk to him."

Sally studied Gary's face and saw only a genial friendliness there. He was trying to help her and she would be silly to refuse his help. The Boyce family needed money too badly. "All right, I'll go with you, Gary."

"Smart girl!" he applauded her. "We have to make some sacrifices to get ahead in business."

Sally remembered her promise to Walter that she would speak to Gary about the job he wanted. But she hesitated to add to her burden of gratitude.

"I'm always glad to help you, Sally," Gary said softly. "You must never hesitate to ask me for anything you want."

"I'm worried about Walter," she said soberly. "He's becoming so discouraged with the insurance business."

Gary took her hands in his, smiling faintly. "And you want me to find him a job in my business?"

"If you could," she said, wanting to withdraw her hands and knowing that she must not.

Gary's eyes were glowing. "I'll put him to work Monday morning, Sally. There isn't anything I wouldn't do for you."

CHAPTER 12

The Whip Cracks

Standing there on the dark veranda with Gary Neylands, Sally was uneasily aware of the glow in his eyes, of the tight grip of his hands on her own. He had helped her to sell cars; he had offered to help her father; he had just promised to give Walter a job. But now she sensed that he was going to draw her into his embrace, to demand payment.

Gary released her hands and stepped back. "You are such a lovely person, Sally. Lovely enough to turn any man's head. I have to keep reminding myself that you are engaged to Walter."

"Yes, I am engaged to Walter," Sally said quietly. "I would do anything to help him."

"Lucky Walter," Gary said tonelessly.

"He needs help so badly, and there is so little I can do for him," she said, and then added eagerly, "I know that he will do well with you, Gary. Walter just isn't the type to make a success of selling."

"There are plenty of men who need a guiding hand," Gary said blandly. "Walter isn't the only one here tonight. Jeff Rainey is another of the same sort."

Sally smiled at the idea. "They are as different as daylight and darkness."

"Both of them are impractical," Gary insisted. "Jeff has ideas, but most of them are worthless."

"My father wouldn't agree with you," Sally said lightly.

Gary laughed a little. "But your father is a sick man now, and his judgment is apt to be faulty."

"Jeff seems to think that Dad is going to help him," she said laughing.

Gary's eyes were grim. "Jeff will have to come to me sooner or later. I'm the only man in this part of the country who manufactures auto accessories."

Sally didn't want to discuss Jeff Rainey, and so she moved toward the door.

"Tell Walter to come to the plant at nine Monday morning," Gary said as they entered the living room.

"I'll tell him," Sally agreed. She saw Walter coming toward her, his face wearing a frown, and was glad when Gary strolled away. Walter came to a stop before her, staring down at her.

"Where have you been, Sally?" I've been looking for you everywhere."

Sally put her hand on his arm, ignoring his tone. "I've some good news for you, Walter. But I shan't tell you what it is until later."

They moved on into the room and Jeff Rainey and Carol Putnam came to join them.

"Jeff and I are going home," Carol announced, smiling at Sally. "Jeff claims that he can't sell cars unless he gets plenty of sleep."

Gary Neylands strolled up with Louise Ives. He glanced at Jeff, smiling blandly. "I'd like to see you sometime next week, Jeff."

"Would you?" Jeff said politely.

Gary nodded. "I have a proposition I think would interest you," he said expansively.

Jeff grinned at him. "You'll forgive me if I doubt it?"

Sally looked at Gary. His face was an expressionless mask, but she knew somehow that he was angered by Jeff's manner.

Gary shrugged. "It won't cost you anything to listen to my proposition, Jeff."

Jeff shook his head; his smile was mocking. "You're a slick talker, Gary. I think I'd better keep away from you."

Sally saw a tiny muscle jerk in Gary's cheek and knew that he was furious. But his voice gave no hint of it.

"You'll listen to me sooner or later, Jeff. And when you do, I'll make some money for you."

"And ten times as much for yourself," Jeff said good-humoredly.

"Is this a dinner party or a business conference?" Carol Putnam asked, laughing.

"Please forgive me, Carol," Gary said suavely. He went with them to the front door and was his genial self again. He gave Sally a small intimate smile just before she and Walter left. "Don't forget that you are paying golf with me tomorrow morning, Sally."

Walter was silent until he turned the roadster into the main highway; then he looked at Sally, scowling. "Are you going to play golf with Gary tomorrow?"

Sally explained it very patiently. "I can't afford to miss a chance to sell a car, Walter. I don't want to play golf with him, but I couldn't refuse."

Walter's lips were twisted. "Of course not! When Gary cracks the whip, we have to jump."

"I wonder if we do have to jump," she said resentfully. "Can't we just forget that we ever met Gary Neylands . . . and go on from there?"

"There are times when I'd like to break his neck," Walter growled.

"Jeff Rainey refuses his help," Sally said uneasily. "I don't see why we couldn't do the same."

"Jeff isn't getting anywhere," Walter pointed out. "And he won't get anywhere unless he listens to Gary."

Sally found herself wondering about this. She had a queer feeling that Jeff would rise in the world without much help from anyone else. "Dad seems to think very highly of Jeff's ideas," she said in a moment.

"Jeff and his ideas!" Walter sneered.

Sally felt an impelling urge to come to the defense of her father's judgment. "Jeff told Dad about one of his ideas the other night, and Dad thought it was wonderful."

Walter drove silently for a minute, then he asked, "What was the idea, Sally?"

Sally explained to him Jeff's plan for a radiator, and gas tank, cap and saw that Walter was interested in spite of himself. But when she had finished, she had an uneasy feeling that she should not have told him. "You mustn't repeat it to anyone else," she cautioned him. "Jeff told Dad in confidence."

"It isn't worth repeating," he scoffed.

Sally smiled at him. "Do you want to hear some good news?" And when he looked at her blankly, "Gary wants you to go to work at the plant Monday morning."

"Do you mean it?" Walter gasped.

Sally nodded, pleased because he was pleased. But she would have felt better, she realized, if he had found a job with someone else. "He didn't say what the job was, Walter. But I'm sure he will give you a good one." Walter was silent and Sally glanced at him. Had it occurred to him that this job would make their marriage possible?

"My mother will be delighted," Walter burst out happily.

Sally knew that Mrs. Norris still had an income. It was very small but enough to keep her. Surely Walter could see that they need wait no longer.

"I wish you had asked Gary what kind of job it is," Walter said doubtfully. "He's always been so vague with me."

Sally leaned back against the cushions, sighing. "I believe Gary will give you a good job."

"If it isn't a good job, I won't accept it," Walter declared. "I'm tired of working for nothing."

Sally closed her eyes wearily. "You can't expect to start at the top, Walter."

"Oh, can't I?" Walter said sarcastically. He was resentfully silent until they reached her house; his goodnight kiss was perfunctory.

And Sally, climbing the stairs, wished passionately that she had never heard of Gary Neylands. Mr. Boyce called to her as she reached his door; and Sally entered the room, trying to look more cheerful than she felt.

"Have a nice time, dear?" he asked.

Sally nodded, smiling. "Splendid!" He patted the edge of the bed invitingly, and she sank down. "You should have been asleep long ago, Dad." His face was pale, his eyes lack-luster; and her thoughts turned unwillingly to Jeff Rainey, who knew how to bring color into her father's face, a sparkle to his eyes.

"I couldn't sleep," Mr. Boyce said tiredly. "In fact, I haven't slept well for several nights."

"Would you like to have me read to you?"

He shook his head. "I tried to read, but I can't find anything that interests me."

Sally remembered her promise to Gary. "It might be good for you to have an occasional visitor, Dad."

His pale face brightened. "You mean . . . Jeff?"

"I was thinking of Gary Neylands. He wants to see you as soon as you are well enough to see anyone."

The brightness faded from his thin face; he shook his head. "I don't care to see Gary Neylands, Sally."

"Gary has been very kind to you, Dad. I don't see why you should refuse to see him."

"I've never had any dealings with Gary," he told her, frowning. "To tell you the truth, he hasn't a very good business reputation. He's too . . . well, ruthless."

"Perhaps less successful men started that rumor," Sally suggested, but her father shook his head stubbornly.

"You may be right. However, I don't want to see him. I neither like nor trust him." Sylvester Boyce sighed. "I can't understand why Jeff doesn't visit me again."

Sally's sigh echoed his. She had been afraid their conversation would lead up to this. "Perhaps Jeff has been busy," she evaded.

His tired, hopeless eyes touched her face. "I always felt better after seeing Jeff. Do you suppose you could persuade him to visit me again, Sally?"

She rose to her feet, managed a smile. "I'll ask him," she promised.

CHAPTER 13

Financial Straits

Sally sat in Philip Ulmer's office Monday morning, listening to his praise, and wondered why she should feel so gloomy.

She had played golf yesterday with Gary Neylands and his friends, Fred Swift and wife, and Swift had given her an order for a Duluth to be delivered today.

"Jeff will have to look to his laurels," Philip Ulmer was saying.

Sally managed a rather sober smile. The prospect of out-selling Jeff Rainey, she confessed, should make her feel happier. But it didn't, and she searched her heart for the reason.

"You have done remarkably well," Ulmer said, smiling, "considering that this is your first attempt at selling, and your first week in the auto sales business."

Sally sighed—and felt guilty for sighing. A week ago, she had asked of life only that she might make a living for her parents and that Walter might get a good job. Now she was making that living and Walter had gone to work today-for Gary Neylands.

Gary Neylands! Sally frowned as her thoughts toyed with that name. Her obligation to the man was mounting by leaps and bounds. Every sale she had made was practically a gift from Gary. Only Carol Putnam's tentative order had come without Gary's help, and that had tumbled into her lap without effort on her part.

"I was afraid at first that you wouldn't do so well," Ulmer said, and studied her face. "Do you mind if I speak plainly, Sally?"

Sally shook her head, puzzled. "Of course not."

"First, let me tell you that I believe your father to be the soul of honor." He cleared his throat and continued. "But banking is different from other businesses. If I should go bankrupt, no one in Avondale would suspect that I was anything but honest. But if I were the president of a bank, and my bank closed, everyone in Avondale would label me a crook."

Sally's heart felt tight as she thought of her father. He was a victim of this very human foible. He had impoverished himself and his family in a vain effort to pay his bank's obligations. He had failed and the failure had broken his heart, because he knew that the town had condemned him.

"Frankly, Sally, I was afraid that you would not be able to sell cars in Avondale," Ulmer said, smiling. "I'm delighted that you are proving me wrong."

Sally rose to her feet. She couldn't very well tell him that she owed her success so far to Gary Neylands. Couldn't tell him that the fruits of success were bitter in her mouth.

"You can see Jeff about getting a demonstrator," Ulmer called after her, as she moved toward the door.

When Sally entered the display room, Jeff was busy with a prospect, a foppish little man wearing a huge diamond ring. She sank into a chair and faced the new business week gloomily. She could expect to sell Carol Putnam a car, but aside from Carol, she had no other prospects in view. Sally thought of her father's quiet declaration that he neither liked nor trusted Gary Neylands. She knew that her father was not aware of their financial straits, but she felt sure that he would refuse help from Gary. Which meant that they must accept Gary's loan—if they did accept it—without her father's knowledge.

"Mustn't start the new week with a gloomy face, Sally."

Sally raised startled, resentful eyes to Jeff Rainey. She noticed that the little man with the diamond ring had vanished.

"Did you let him get away?" she asked.

Jeff smiled ruefully. "He allowed me to know that he liked nothing about the Duluth or about me. I thought of breaking his neck, but I was afraid you might be shocked."

Sally remembered that she had felt rather kindly toward Jeff yesterday, that she had defended him to Walter Saturday night. It puzzled her now that she could have been so silly. Jeff's cheerful countenance was a distinct affront. Life wasn't a joke and he had no right to consider it as such. "Mr. Ulmer told me to see you about a demonstrator," she said coldly.

"I'm having one polished and greased for you," Jeff smiled genially. "If you don't sell a car today, it won't be my fault." His eyes were teasing. "Ulmer tells me you sold more cars than I did last week."

Sally searched the blue eyes staring down at her. He simply couldn't be as pleased as he sounded. He must resent it because she, a new salesman, had outsold him.

"You've been doing great so far," Jeff said quietly. "But don't get discouraged if you don't sell a car every day. I've gone as long as a month without selling a car." Jeff turned away. "I'll bring your car around front, Sally."

Sally watched him stride away, watched him until he disappeared through the door leading to the repair department. Then she turned and moved toward the front entrance.

Had Walter been right in saying that Jeff was playing a deep game with the wealthy Carol Putnam? Was Jeff's refusal to sell her a car merely an effort on his part to gain her confidence?

The shining Duluth slid to the curb before her, and Jeff Rainey left the car. He smiled at her as she took his place. "Has Gary lined up any more prospects for you, Sally?" he asked, eyes twinkling.

Sally had hoped that no one else would notice that she owed her sales to Gary. She slammed the door, gave Jeff a cold glance. "Are you jealous of my sales, Mr. Rainey?" She was pleased to see a faint color steal into his lean cheeks.

Jeff shook his head, smiling again. "No, I'm not jealous, Miss Boyce," he said easily.

Angrily Sally threw the car into gear. And not until she had driven blindly for several blocks did she remember that she had forgotten to invite Jeff to visit her father.

~ ~ ~

When Sally reached home that night, she found Walter in the living room with her mother. Mrs. Boyce looked tired and dispirited, but Walter looked more cheerful than usual.

"Do you like your new job?" Sally asked him, sinking wearily into a chair.

Walter shrugged. "It isn't what I hoped for, but it's better than nothing."

"Tell me all about it," Sally urged.

"Forty a week, assistant to the personnel manager." He smiled complacently. "The manger is a dope, so I'll probably get his job before long."

Sally was glad to see that he had regained some of his lost confidence, but wondered uneasily if he wasn't a bit too confident. Gary wasn't the sort of businessman who employed incompetents, and she doubted if the personnel manager was what Walter said. She let it pass, while her thoughts considered the future. If she and her mother decided to accept Gary's loan, then she and Walter could be married at once. But of course, she would continue selling Duluths until her father was well and making a living again.

"I expect to go far in Gary's business," Walter was saying. "I've already suggested some changes to Gary, and he said that he would consider them."

Sally's heart sank. "You mean you went to Gary over the personnel manager's head, Walter?"

Walter looked puzzled. "Why shouldn't I? After all, Gary and I are personal friends, and the personnel manager is an old fogy."

Sally looked at her mother. "How is Dad tonight?"

"He isn't any better," Mrs. Boyce said, her lips trembling. "Dr. Frobisher says he will remain the same unless we take him to that specialist."

Walter rose to his feet. "Gary told me that he was coming here tonight, so I'll run along."

Sally went to the front door with him, "Do be careful, Walter. I'm so anxious for you to make good on your new job."

"I'm going to knock 'em dead out there," he assured her; then he looked away, "I think you should accept that loan from Gary."

His expression told her what she wanted to know, but Sally couldn't resist asking the question. "Did Gary speak to you about it, Walter?"

Walter flushed. "Of course he did. You and I are engaged, and there is every reason why he should consult me."

"I suppose so," Sally agreed dryly, and wondered what the advice Walter would have given if he hadn't been working for Gary. Returning to the living room, Sally felt even gloomier than she had felt during the day. She had made no sales; nor had she talked to anyone who seemed to be interested in buying a Duluth.

Her mother glanced up at her as she entered the room. "Have you decided what answer you will give Mr. Neylands?" Mrs. Boyce asked.

Sally shook her head, sighing. "I don't know what to do, Mother. I hate to go into debt, but I can't bear to see Dad denied the treatment he needs."

"Our duty seems very clear to me," Mrs. Boyce said firmly. "I think that we should accept Mr. Neylands' loan. Sylvester can repay the money when he gets well."

"If he gets well," Sally commented, sighing.

"Dr. Frobisher says that he will, Sally. Surely, we can take his word for it. I think it is high time we faced things honestly, Sally," Mrs. Boyce said quietly. "I think you should break your engagement to Walter."

"Why, Mother!" Sally gasped. "Surely you don't mean that."

"I do mean it," Mrs. Boyce declared. "You must face the fact that he is a failure, and that he will remain one." Her thin face softened a little. "You cannot waste your life on him, dear."

Sally swallowed angrily. "Have you forgotten that Walter loves me, and that I love him?"

"Gary Neylands loves you, too," Mrs. Boyce said gently. "I want you to remember that when he comes here tonight."

"It isn't true!" Sally cried.

CHAPTER 14

Slick Talker

Her mother's declaration that Gary Neylands loved her, left Sally paralyzed with astonishment. Mrs. Boyce nodded and there was a bitter sort of amusement in her eyes. "It is quite true, Sally," she said firmly. "Gary Neylands loves you."

"How can you believe anything so preposterous!" Sally gasped. "Why, he's only been here once."

"Once was enough for me to realize the truth," her mother observed quietly; then her thin lips pressed together, "I'm very glad that he does love you. You have said that you want to re-establish our fortunes. Well, Gary Neylands is the answer to that."

Sally shook her head bewilderedly. "But he doesn't love me!" she cried.

No, she couldn't admit it. Louise Ives might say so and her mother might do the same, but she, Sally, couldn't admit it. Once she admitted that, it would be impossible for her to continue their friendship. Impossible to accept his help for her father!

Mrs. Boyce smiled at her. "You were always such an honest child, dear. I don't believe you will refuse to face the truth."

"It isn't the truth," Sally said obstinately. "He has never shown anything but friendliness for me."

"I don't believe he will, so long as you are engaged to Walter," Mrs. Boyce said. "Which means, of course, that you must break your engagement to Walter."

Sally's teeth met in her trembling lips. "I'll never break my engagement to Walter. It would kill him if I did."

"If you marry Walter," her mother said sharply, "you will learn to hate him."

Sally's eyes widened; she had never seen her mother so in earnest about anything. "I don't understand you, Mother," she said weakly.

Mrs. Boyce was smiling again. "I objected to your selling automobiles, but secretly I was proud of you. We were in serious straits financially, and you met the situation bravely."

"It was the only thing I could do," Sally objected, puzzled.

"Walter hasn't been so brave, darling. He has spent his time complaining instead of working. I'm sure that Gary has given Walter a job simply for your sake, and I can't believe that Walter will hold the job long. Walter was an agreeable and acceptable person before his mother lost most of her money, Sally. Now he is . . . nothing!"

Sally shivered before these blunt words. She rose to her feet, trembling. "Would you want me to marry Gary Neylands, knowing that I don't love him, Mother?"

Mrs. Boyce shook her head, very firmly. "I believe that you are going to fall out of love with Walter. When that happens, I am hoping that your thoughts will turn to Gary Neylands. He is good looking, cultured and wealthy . . . everything that any girl should require in a man."

Sally smiled wryly. "That sounds very reasonable, but the human heart doesn't listen to reason." Then she came to Walter's defense. "Walter can be excused for acting as he does. His mother always babied him. If he has weaknesses, it is her fault."

Mrs. Boyce's quick nod agreed with this. "But there is no reason why you should suffer for his mother's mistakes. Both of you will be unhappy if you get married."

"His mother lost her money through Dad's bank," Sally reminded her mother.

"Are you going to marry him simply because his mother lost her money when our bank collapsed?"

"I love him," Sally said stubbornly, "and I won't desert him . . . ever!"

Later, when she entered her father's bedroom carrying a tray, she thought at first that he was asleep. But his eyes turned slowly to meet her as she crossed the room.

"Something special tonight," Sally smiled. "Real strawberries with real cream."

Mr. Boyce's pallid face showed no interest. "Just set it down on the table. Maybe I can eat it later."

"You are going to eat it now," Sally said with firm tenderness.

She persuaded him, finally, but his listless attack on the appetizing food brought tears to her eyes. When he finished, she moved the tray from the bed. "Do you think you can go to sleep now, Dad?"

Mr. Boyce shook his head. "Not much chance of that, I'm afraid. I haven't done much sleeping for several nights."

Sally searched her mind for some way to make him feel more cheerful. "I'm going to sell a car to Carol Putnam sometime this week," she told him.

"That's nice, Sally." His eyes raised to her face. "How is Jeff getting along?"

Sally's lips felt dry. She hadn't kept her promise to him, about asking Jeff to visit him. "Jeff has been pretty busy," she evaded, "but he is coming to see you soon." And vowed that she would speak to Jeff tomorrow morning, at no matter what cost to her pride.

Mr. Boyce's eyes brightened a little. "He's a fine lad, Sally." He smiled a little. "Jeff makes me believe that I can do what I must do, sooner or later."

"What is that, Dad?"

"Pay off the rest of the bank's obligations. If I could only do that, I think I could die happy."

Sally stirred uneasily. Had he been worrying about this, all those endless days when he stared hopelessly at the ceiling? She had thought that his mind was a blank, that he had no real memory of his troubles.

"You must not think about that now," she said huskily. "There's time enough for that when you are completely recovered."

"Yes, when I am well," he repeated hopelessly.

"Gary Neylands wants you in his business when you are well," Sally said, on the spur of the moment.

"Gary Neylands?" He looked at her blankly, shook his head. "I neither trust nor like the man. I couldn't possibly consider any proposition coming from him."

Sally heard a car stop in front of the house and saw that her father had heard it, too.

"Maybe that's Jeff," he said, smiling.

"I think that Jeff is going to be busy tonight, Dad." She stared at him thoughtfully. "Would you like to have another doctor examine you?"

His thin shoulders lifted. "It doesn't matter, Sally. I'm afraid that no doctor can do much for me."

Sally heard her mother calling her and shivered, knowing that Gary Neylands had come for his answer.

~ ~ ~

Sally found Gary Neylands in the living room, chatting amiably with her mother. He rose to greet her, very distinguished in his dark, well-tailored business suit.

"You are looking very lovely, Sally," he murmured.

Sally searched his face. *Was her mother right? Did this suave young man with the guarded eyes love her?*

"Has Walter been here tonight?" Gary asked.

Sally nodded. "He is delighted with his job. We— we have so much to thank you for."

"You have nothing to thank me for," Gary said easily. "I believe that Walter will make me a valuable man, as soon as he learns the business."

"Walter is so ambitious," she said uneasily. "I hope you won't misunderstand anything he does."

"Don't give it another thought, Sally. I'll push Walter ahead as fast as I possibly can."

Mrs. Boyce rose to her feet, moved toward the hall door. "I want to speak to my husband before he goes to sleep," she told Gary, smiling.

"Have you decided to send him to the specialist?" Gary asked Mrs. Boyce.

Mrs. Boyce looked at Sally, then back to Gary again. "Sally is the business head of our family now, Mr. Neylands. The decision rests with her."

Sally felt a vague resentment as her mother disappeared. Then it came to her that her mother's presence was not really necessary. She knew that her mother wanted her to accept the loan from Gary. Knew that she wanted even more than that.

"Did you have a good day, Sally?" Gary smiled.

Sally shook her head. "I didn't even come close to selling a car."

Gary looked properly sympathetic. "There are days like that in all businesses. You must not let it discourage you." He cleared his throat. "What shall we do about your father, Sally?"

Sally smiled soberly. "I'm finding it hard to make up my mind, Gary. Dad says he doesn't believe another doctor could help him."

Gary nodded his understanding. "It's natural that he should feel like that, Sally. But of course, we can't allow sick people to make decisions for themselves. If we did, few of them would ever get well."

He was so reasonable—so darned reasonable! Sally thought wearily and remembered what Jeff had said at Gary's dinner party: "You are a slick talker, Gary. I think I'd better stay away from you."

Jeff Rainey seemed to fill her thoughts suddenly—his rumpled sandy hair, his stubborn jaw, his laughing blue eyes, his carefree smile, his courage. Yes, that was it—courage. Jeff's pockets were empty, but he had ideas and courage. Courage enough to face his problems and try to solve them himself. Courage enough so that he refused to sell a car to a girl, knowing that she loved him.

"You have been very kind to me, Gary," she heard herself saying in a voice that sounded strange to her. "But I feel that I must solve my own problems in the future."

Gary Neylands' lips were smiling, but there was no humor in his eyes. He rose to his feet. "Am I to take this as final?" he asked quietly.

CHAPTER 15

Braver and Stronger

The ensuing week passed much too swiftly for Sally. When she arrived home Friday night, only an effort of will made it possible for her to maintain a cheerful countenance. She had sold no more Duluths during the week, nor had she any live prospects in view.

"I haven't sold a car," she thought with a wry smile, "since I told Gary Neylands that I wanted to settle my own problems in the future." And called herself foolish for thinking of Gary in this connection. He couldn't be blamed for her failure to sell Duluths. She had known all along, she told herself sternly, that she couldn't expect his continued assistance. She was giving herself a manicure when she heard Walter's car stop in front of the house.

"How about a kiss for a big shot in the auto accessories business, Sally?"

Sally raised her lips to him, her heart swelling with happiness and relief. "I'm so glad you are doing so well, Walter," she said fervently.

Walter's face clouded a little. "Did you have doubts about it?"

Sally shrugged. "Anything can happen."

Walter smiled complacently. "Gary is shifting me into another department next week. He wants me to learn all angles of the business. I feel sure that he has a big job in view for me." His smile broadened. "Let's take in a movie, just to celebrate."

"Let's," Sally agreed, laughing. She heard another car stop before the house and her laughter was stilled. She had humbled her pride, and Jeff Rainey had visited her father twice during the week. But not even the noticeable improvement in her father's appearance could make her enjoy these visits. She opened the door at Jeff's knock and gave him a polite smile as he entered.

Jeff's genial salutation elicited no more than a mutter from Walter, but Jeff appeared not to notice. "How is your father?" he asked Sally.

"He looks some better," Sally admitted, and studied his face, wondering what there was about him to make Sylvester Boyce feel braver and stronger.

Jeff grinned at her. "The eminent Dr. Jefferson Rainey is always successful with his patients," he said grandly.

Sally found her lips wavering into a smile, in response to that contagious grin of his.

Walter growled, "I suppose you think you are doing the Boyces a big favor by coming here?"

Sally frowned at him; she had explained the reason for these visits, and he had no right to speak like that.

"I like Sylvester Boyce," Jeff said easily, "but I must admit that my visits are not entirely unselfish."

"I thought you had something up your sleeve," Walter said unpleasantly.

Sally said hurriedly, "I think we'd better run along, Walter." She saw that Jeff's smile was gone, that his hands had suddenly become fists.

"A good idea," Jeff said softly. "Otherwise I might be tempted to demonstrate what I've got up my sleeve."

"What do you mean by that crack?" Walter asked pugnaciously.

"Hurry, Walter," Sally said uneasily. "I don't like to be late to a movie."

Jeff's smile was in place again; he glanced at Walter. "I understand there is a good job open at the Phoenix Plow Works, Walter. You might get a job there."

Walter scowled at him. "Thanks for nothing! I've got a job at Gary Neylands' plant."

Jeff shrugged. "Just thought I'd mention it." Jeff turned and began mounting the stairs, three steps at a time.

~ ~ ~

"I'm going to take a poke at that fellow someday," Walter growled, as they were driving toward town.

Sally considered this without any pleasure. She had no doubt but what Walter would come out second-best in a physical encounter with Jeff Rainey. Jeff had to fight his way through life, while Walter's way had been made easy with his mother's money.

"I don't believe I would do that," she advised quietly, and found herself wondering what Jeff had meant by telling Walter about the job at the plow works. Walter was doing well where he was and there was no reason why he should make a change.

Presently she found something else to puzzle about. What had Jeff meant when he admitted that he had selfish reasons for calling on her father? Sylvester Boyce had no money and could not finance Jeff's ideas, even if he wanted to.

"Gary doesn't like it very well because you refused to accept that loan from him." Walter told her suddenly.

"Has he said anything to you, Walter?"

"Gary mentioned it today."

Sally smiled ruefully. "Did you tell him that I haven't sold any more Duluths?"

Walter nodded, frowning. "It doesn't pay to alienate your friends, Sally. You should have accepted that loan from Gary."

"I don't agree with you," Sally said resentfully. "Sooner or later, everyone must learn to stand on his own feet."

"That sounds very pretty," Walter scoffed, "but it isn't the way of modern business. You can't get anywhere unless you have influential friends. And you must not be too proud to accept their help."

~ ~ ~

Leaving the office of one Alexander Butler, the following afternoon, Sally was almost inclined to agree with what Walter had said last night. Driving slowly through town in a highly polished demonstrator, she gave herself up to gloomy reflections. The clock on the dash informed her that it was mid-afternoon; and that soon she must return to Ulmer's and admit to herself that her week's effort had been wasted.

Sally was beginning to realize that her name had something do with her failure. Several of her prospects had shown an interest until they had come to realize that she was Sylvester Boyce's daughter. Then their interest had waned. There were tears of discouragement in her eyes when, presently, they fell on a huge sign: "Adolph Gingrich Wholesale Plumbing Company." Her feeling of discouragement turned quickly to one of anger. It was people like Gingrich, she thought wrathfully, who were the cause of her discouragement. An idea, like a flame, licked across her mind suddenly. She guided the car to the curb, threw on the brake, and sat there for a moment nibbling on a forefinger.

Adolph Gingrich looked up as Sally entered his office. His mouth fell open, and he gave a gusty, incredulous grunt. "You!" he whispered throatily.

Sally fixed him with a purposeful glance. "I've come to sell you a Duluth," she announced.

Gingrich swallowed noisily; his eyebrows twitched. "You've come to sell me a Duluth?" he repeated blankly.

Sally listened for a moment to her frightened heart, then told herself that he couldn't do any worse than kill her. "Yes, I've come to sell you a Duluth," she said firmly.

Gingrich peered past her toward the door. "I suppose you've got your boyfriend outside," he sneered. "You wouldn't dare come here alone."

Boyfriend? She didn't understand him for a moment, then she flushed as she thought of Jeff Rainey. "He isn't my boyfriend, and I did come alone," she said angrily. "I'm not afraid of you."

Gingrich's round head wagged unbelievingly. "You slapped my face, and yet you dare come here again?"

"The Duluth automobile," Sally said in a voice that wavered in spite of her best efforts, "is by far the best car on the market for anywhere near the same money."

Gingrich sucked in a noisy breath. "Git!" he snarled.

"This is bargain day on Duluths, Mr. Gingrich."

His angry eyes searched hers. "What do you mean?"

"You were interested in a Duluth a week ago, weren't you?" Sally wheeled.

"I'm not interested any longer," Gingrich snarled. "You can't slap my face, and then sell me a car." He glared at her silently for a moment, then asked suspiciously, "What do you mean by a bargain?"

"I'll sell you a Duluth car today," Sally told him, "at the regular price less my commission."

"Less your commission?" Gingrich repeated in a puzzled voice. "I don't get it."

"It's very simple," Sally explained, encouraged by his interest. "If you will buy a Duluth from me, I'll write you a check for the amount of my commission. In other words, I'll make nothing on the sale."

Gingrich's chair squeaked as he leaned back, surveying her with suspicious, puzzled eyes. "I still don't get it. Why should you do me a favor?"

"I want you to apply the amount of my commission toward what Dad—or rather the bank—still owes you. It's just my way of helping pay Dad's debts."

"But he doesn't owe me anything, legally," Gingrich growled.

"We expect to pay it, anyway," Sally said stiffly.

"How much is your commission?" he asked, and when she told him, he leaned toward her, scowling. "I think you're bluffing. I don't believe a Boyce will do something for nothing."

"Try me and see," Sally invited happily. "I can take you to Ulmer's now, and we can conclude the deal."

Gingrich jerked to his feet; he scowled at her as he circled the desk. "Let's go, Miss Boyce. I'm calling your bluff."

CHAPTER 16

In Need of a Slap

It was six o'clock when Sally concluded her deal with Adolph Gingrich; and not until she had given him a check for her commission and watched him drive away in a new Duluth, did she allow herself to believe that she had gotten away with it. Sally's legs felt weak as she turned and retraced her steps to Philip Ulmer's office. She sank into a chair and Ulmer turned puzzled eyes on her.

"How in the world did you manage it, Sally?" he asked.

She explained the deal to Ulmer, adding, "I should have asked you first, but I couldn't see why you should object."

Ulmer's face still held that puzzled look. "But your father doesn't legally owe Mr. Gingrich anything, Sally," he protested. "Your father's creditors took everything he had."

"Dad will feel responsible so long as a dollar of it remains unpaid," Sally told him. Then she asked, "Do you object to my selling cars on that basis?"

Ulmer shrugged. "Why should I? I get my profit just the same." He leaned back in his chair, staring at her curiously. "I still find it hard to believe that you sold Gingrich." Ulmer gave her an admiring twinkling glance. "Perhaps it pays to have red hair after all. I wonder what Jeff will think when he hears about this."

Sally laughed. She hadn't seen Jeff since early morning and hoped that he would return before she left. She could picture his amazement when he learned of her sale.

The telephone shrilled and Ulmer answered it; then pushed the instrument toward her. "This is Gary Neylands, Sally."

Her eager anticipation gave way to dread. Was something wrong with Walter? Had he been fired? She managed to give him a fairly steady greeting. "How is Walter getting along?" she asked.

"He seems to be doing pretty well," Gary told her, but his voice lacked enthusiasm. Then he asked, "Have you been selling any cars recently, Sally?"

"I've been doing pretty well," Sally said blandly. "I just sold a car to a man named Adolph Gingrich."

"That's nice, Sally," Gary said tonelessly. "Glad to hear you are doing well."

But there was something in his voice that made her wonder if he really was glad; and she was puzzled by the purpose of his call.

"I was wondering if you wouldn't like to play golf with me again tomorrow?" Gary said.

"I'm sorry, Gary," Sally said kindly, "but I promised Walter that I would go swimming with him tomorrow."

Gary was silent for a moment, giving her time to wonder what would be the result of her refusal. Would he be angry? And would he vent his anger on her—or on Walter?

Gary sounded undisturbed. "I suppose I'll see you at the country club dance tonight, Sally?"

"Of course," Sally replied, and called herself silly for believing that he would be angered by anything so unimportant. She was setting the phone down when the office door burst open and Jeff Rainey strode into the room.

He gave Ulmer a frowning glance, ignoring Sally. "Did you know that one of your cars has been stolen?" Jeff asked Ulmer.

"One of our cars stolen!" Ulmer repeated, and shook his head. "No, I didn't know it."

"It's a fact," Jeff declared, and looked at Sally. "Do you remember that Gingrich fellow, whose ugly face you slapped?"

Sally nodded, suppressing a smile; she was beginning to understand. "Yes, I remember him, Jeff."

"I just passed him out on South Boulevard. He was hitting seventy in a new Duluth." Jeff scratched his head puzzledly. "It's darn funny. Gingrich has plenty of money. Can't understand why he should steal a car."

Ulmer exchanged a bland glance with Sally. "Maybe we'd better get in touch with the police," he said grinning.

Sally's mirth got the best of her, and Jeff Rainey stared at her suspiciously. His suspicious eyes went to Ulmer when he saw that she was incapable of speaking. "What's the joke?" Jeff demanded.

Ulmer chuckled. "Sally sold Gingrich a new Duluth, Jeff."

Jeff's knees buckled, and he leaned weakly against the desk. He spread an incredulous glance between them. "Tell me another!" he growled. Ulmer passed him Gingrich's contract and Jeff's eyes flicked over it widening. He looked at Sally. "You sold that gorilla a car?" he whispered.

Sally nodded, grinning. "Why not?"

Jeff slapped the contract down, glared at her. "That's Gingrich's signature, all right," Jeff conceded. "I sold him a car myself one time." He choked a little. "But how did you do it, Sally?"

Sally moved toward the door. "It isn't hard to sell cars," she purred sweetly, "when you know how." She heard his footsteps behind her as she crossed the deserted display room; and he caught up with her at the front entrance.

"Just a minute, Sally," Jeff begged. "If you don't explain how you sold Gingrich, I'm liable to explode."

Sally allowed herself to be detained. Jeff's look of bewilderment, which gave way to one of admiration, as she explained, was very pleasant to see.

When she had finished, Jeff nodded soberly. "It took courage to go back to see Gingrich, Sally."

Sally was finding it possible tonight to feel friendly toward everyone, even toward Jeff Rainey who said and did so many irritating things. Which reminded her of something. "I want you to explain something to me, Jeff."

Jeff stared at her curiously. "Name it."

"Why did you tell Walter about that job at the plow works?"

Jeff's eyes narrowed. "I'd rather not explain that."

Sally frowned at him. "I would like to know your reason . . . if you had one."

Jeff hesitated. "I just thought Walter might do better working for another firm." He smiled a little. "But you must remember that I don't like Gary Neylands."

There was something in his manner, rather than in his words, that made her feel resentful. "Why should Walter do better elsewhere?" she demanded.

"I'd rather not talk about it, Sally."

"Are you afraid to tell me?"

Jeff's mouth tightened. "You're asking for it, Sally—" He broke off, turning away.

"Wait!" she said angrily, and when he turned again, "I demand that you tell me."

Jeff shrugged resignedly. "In my opinion, Gary gave Walter a job just to please you."

Sally's fingers curled. Jeff Rainey had a face that badly needed slapping.

Jeff said grimly, "If you slap me, Sally Boyce, I'll shake the breath out of you."

Sally was furious, but not too furious to read in his eyes that he would undoubtedly shake the breath out of her if she slapped him. Her fingers uncurled—reluctantly. "How dare you say such a thing!" she gasped, and remembered miserably that Walter had gone to work for Gary only after she had asked it.

"You demanded my opinion, and you got it," Jeff snapped.

Sally's eyes blazed at him. "I hate you!" And felt that the blue eyes staring at her were growing wider and wider, consuming her. She was drowning in their blue depths.

"I wonder if you do?" Jeff said softy.

~ ~ ~

Seated in the living room that night, waiting for Walter's arrival, Sally decided that it had been a successful and pleasant day. She found herself wondering, while half listening to her mother's idle chatter, why Jeff Rainey made her so furious. Now that she was calm again, she had to admit that she had asked for his opinion, so there had been no reason for the fury that had gripped her.

Walter's knock sent her running to the door. But when she saw his face, her throat tightened. "Why, what's wrong, dear?" she asked anxiously.

"I'll tell you on the way to the club," he said gruffly.

Hurriedly, Sally got a wrap and bade her mother goodnight. When they were in Walter's car, she turned to him. "You look positively sick, Walter. Tell me about it."

Walter gave her a quick, scowling glance. "Gary has shifted me to another department," he began, and seemed to choke on his resentment.

"But Gary said that he might do that. You must not resent it, dear."

Walter's barking laugh made her shiver. "But he's cut my salary in half. I'm to get twenty dollars next week."

"He cut you from forty to twenty dollars?" Sally murmured aghast. "But what reason did he give?"

"Oh, he gave a darn good reason," Walter sneered. "Says he intends to shift me from one job to another, but that I must take whatever salary goes with each job."

Sally's heart sank as she stared into the night. Gary had called her at six o'clock and had not mentioned this. "When did Gary tell you this?" she asked.

"I didn't get away from the plant until seven o'clock," Walter replied. "He told me just before I left."

Sally bit her lip. Gary had asked her for a date at six o'clock. She had reused, and, at seven o'clock, he had cut Walter's salary in half.
"Gary is sore at us because you wouldn't let him help your father," Walter complained.

CHAPTER 17

The Embrace

Sally felt Walter's hand tighten on her arm when they entered the ballroom at the country club.

"There's Carruth Wade with Carol Putnam," he whispered.

The couple was strolling toward them and Sally returned Carol's friendly smile, but she braced herself to meet Carruth Wade. He was Avondale's most powerful man, both financially and politically. He was too wealthy to be seriously hurt by the collapse of one bank, but Sally knew that he had been the biggest single loser when her father's bank closed its doors.

"I'm delighted with my car," Carol said enthusiastically. "I'm boosting the Duluth to all my friends."

Sally thanked her and waited rather breathlessly for Carruth Wade to speak. This was the first time she had seen him since the bank failed, and she believed he would be distinctly cool. But Wade was smiling now, and his gray eyes held a friendly light.

"I've been hearing things about you, Sally," Wade said, smiling. "I hear that you are selling Duluths at bargain prices."

"Who told you about it?" Sally smiled.

"Two or three people have mentioned it. Is it true?"

Sally admitted it was true, and feeling Walter's hand tighten on her arm again, remembered that she had forgotten to tell him about it.

Wade's eyes were twinkling. "You might see me at my office the latter part of next week. I never could resist a bargain." Then he asked gravely, "How is Sylvester getting along?"

"Dad seems to be better," Sally replied, and was forced, unwillingly, to think of Jeff Rainey. Her eyes moved over the ballroom, but she didn't see Jeff and decided that she might expect to have a pleasant evening.

"This rest will be good for your father," Wade was saying, and then he smiled again. "I've often thought of having a nervous breakdown myself. It's my one chance for a needed rest."

Sally's shining eyes followed them as they moved away. Carol liked her Duluth and was boosting it to her friends. Carruth Wade wasn't bitter about his loss, and he had invited her to call on him about a Duluth.

"What's this about selling Duluths at bargain prices?" Walter asked.

Sally smiled at him. "If you lost money through Dad's bank, you can buy a Duluth at a bargain price. When you buy the car, I give you a check for my commission." Walter's expression said that her explanation just didn't make sense.

"You give the buyer your commission and then Ulmer pays you the commission," he repeated, puzzledly. "But you only break even on the deal, Sally. You don't make a cent."

"Einstein had better look to his laurels," Sally teased.

Gary Neylands and Louise Ives approached them, and Sally braced herself again. But both of them seemed to be in a genial humor.

"May I borrow Sally for one dance?" Gary asked Walter.

Walter shrugged, scowling. "Why not?" he said ungraciously.

Dancing with Gary, Sally heard his quiet chuckle. "I'm afraid Walter isn't liking me tonight," he said.

"Walter is feeling discouraged," Sally said stiffly. "He had hoped to do well at your plant."

"I was afraid that Walter wouldn't understand my action," Gary said quietly. "But I felt sure that you would."

Sally raised a puzzled face to him. "But you were paying him forty dollars a week, and you've cut him to twenty. It seems to me that he has a right to feel discouraged."

"And I thought you had such a good business brain," Gary sighed, smiling down at her.

His smile disconcerted her, made her wonder if she had jumped too quickly to the wrong conclusion. "It appears to be a very simple problem in mathematics," she said defensively.

"Appears to be, is right," Gary chuckled. Then he asked playfully, "Shall I explain myself, or would you rather be angry with me?"

With his smiling face before her, Sally had an uneasy feeling that she had been foolish. Gary had called her at six o'clock asking her for a date. She had refused and an hour later he had cut Walter's salary in half. She had concluded that the two were related, that Gary's treatment of Walter had resulted from his anger toward her. "You don't owe me an explanation," she told him. "But I would like to hear it."

"Then I'll start by reminding you that Walter knows nothing about the manufacturing of automobile accessories," Gary said genially.

"I understand that much," Sally smiled faintly.

"Since he knows nothing about it, he must be given a chance to learn. Is that clear, too?"

"Quite clear," Sally replied, returning his smile.

"We have dozens of departments at the plant," Gary continued more soberly. "I want Walter to understand the operations in all of them, and he can learn this only by working in them."

"That sounds very reasonable," Sally said, and heard a mocking voice in her brain, say, "You're a slick talker, Gary!"

"The only objectionable feature," Gary was saying, "is that Walter must be satisfied with whatever salary goes with each job."

Sally decided that she was convinced, but she wondered doubtfully if Walter could be persuaded that Gary's plan was reasonable.

Gary asked, smiling, "What's this I hear about you selling Duluths at bargain prices, Sally?"

Sally was amazed at the speed with which news traveled in Avondale. "Who told you about it?" she asked curiously.

"None other than Adolph Gingrich," Gary laughed, "so you needn't deny it."

"I don't want to deny it," Sally retorted. "I'm proud of my plan."

"You have a right to be proud," Gary said sincerely. "It's quite the nicest thing I've ever heard of."

His praise brought color to her cheeks, made her ashamed that she had doubted his kindness, his generosity.

"The average person wouldn't have thought of such a plan," Gary continued gravely. "And even if he had, he would have rejected it, because there is no profit in it."

Walter and Louise danced past them, and Sally got a fleeting glimpse of their faces. Louise was staring at him with adoring eyes, and Walter seemed to have forgotten his troubles.

"I understand that you have competition, Sally," Gary said, and his twinkling eyes said that he had noticed Louise and Walter, too.

"So I understand," Sally said lightly. "But it takes two to make a bargain."

"You seem to be very sure of Walter," Gary commented quickly.

Sally searched his eyes, prepared to be angry, but his expression showed nothing but a friendly interest. "As sure as I am of life itself, Gary."

"I think I would find life very dull if I were sure of everything," Gary replied, then he asked, "Is your father getting along all right?"

Sally was reminded of his proffered loan and of her refusal. Was reminded that her father was looking better and of the reason for it. Darn Jeff Rainey!

"Dad seems to be a lot better."

"Glad to hear it. Does Jeff still visit him?"

"Yes."

Gary looked thoughtful. "Do you suppose your father and Jeff are planning to form a partnership?"

Sally shrugged. "They don't confide in me."

"If they do," Gary continued, smiling, "I wonder what they intend to use for money?"

Her belief wavered suddenly. Jeff Rainey was a stubbornly determined person. He might accomplish something, where a less-determined person would fail. She remembered her last furious encounter with him, remembered his whispered threat: "If you slap me . . . I'll shake the breath out of you!" She wondered, dizzily, how it would feel to have the breath shaken out of you by Jeff Rainey.

"Did I say something to anger you, Sally?" Gary was asking.

Sally started, then put a finger to her temple and found a strong pulse beating there. "A sudden headache," she explained.

"Perhaps a breath of air would be good for you," Gary said solicitously. "It is rather stuffy in here."

Sally wondered miserably if fresh air were a cure for silly memories. She decided that it might be, and so she murmured an agreement and walked with Gary across the dance floor and through a door to the veranda. It was dark there and cool and pale stars were visible through the trees, and Sally thought that she would feel better in a moment. But she felt a growing uneasiness as she strolled along with Gary—that same uneasiness she always felt when alone with him. They turned a corner and Sally's heart and feet came to a sudden stop, as she saw the two who stood before her, locked in a tight embrace. Her amazed gasp brought them apart.

Louise Ives laughed coolly, smiling coquettishly at Walter. "Can't one find privacy anywhere?" Louise complained lightly.

"Sally!" Walter Norris whispered.

CHAPTER 18

Squabbling Girls

Staring at Walter and Louise, Sally felt the blood drain from her heart. She had known that Walter was weak and that Louise was determined to get him. But not for an instant had she suspected that Walter would succumb to Louise's rather obvious wiles. But she could not deny the evidence of her senses, could not deny that she had seen them, a moment ago, locked tightly in each other's arms.

Louise glanced at Walter and her laughter tinkled. "It must be a nuisance to have a fianc□e who follows you around so closely, Walter."

"Sally and I were not following anybody," Gary Neylands interposed quietly. "She had a headache and we decided that fresh air might make her feel better. We didn't know you two were out here."

Sally felt grateful to him for putting into words what her numb lips could not utter. But gratitude could not live long in the flame of the sick anger that consumed her. She ignored Walter's entreating eyes, turned to Gary. "Shall we return to the ballroom?"

"If you wish."

She took his arm and they strolled back the way they had come. Sally's anger was giving place to panic. The world had gone crazy beginning with the collapse of the Citizens Bank.

"You mustn't take this too much to heart," Gary said gently. "Louise is a very attractive girl, and Walter is—well—"

Sally finished it for him, in a choked voice. "Weak!"

"All men are weak in some way," Gary said oracularly. "So you must not condemn Walter for his moment of weakness."

"You might not find it so easy to forgive, if it had happened to you," she said angrily.

Gary took one of her hands in his, patted it gently. "I think you should give Walter a chance to explain, Sally."

"Explain!" Sally flared. "All the explaining in the world can't make me forget what I saw."

Gary appeared to be very thoughtful. "Perhaps Walter feels too sure of you, Sally." He smiled rather grimly. "You are not expert at hiding your feelings."

"I have wanted Walter to feel sure of me; just as I wanted to feel sure of him." Her voice broke. "It's all we have left to feel sure of."

Gary shook his head. "Men don't appreciate certainties. They like to be kept guessing."

"I don't believe it," Sally said miserably.

Gary smiled at her, as at a child who is being willfully unreasonable. "You have given Walter the right to believe that you will not abandon him, no matter what he does, no matter what happens to him." His shoulders lifted. "Do you think it is wise, Sally?"

"I don't know what you mean."

"Most girls, under the same circumstances, would have abandoned Walter long ago. They would have decided to make a more advantageous marriage."

"But I didn't decide that and I never will!" Sally said, and shuddered as her thoughts conjured up a picture of Walter holding Louise in his arms, oblivious of everything but her lips pressed to his. Was it possible, then, to forgive anything?

"Your attitude is admirable, provided you don't let Walter know about it," Gary smiled. "He wouldn't be human if he didn't take advantage of it."

Sally's thoughts moved confusedly. Was Gary speaking the truth? Had she allowed Walter to believe that she would stand just anything from him? Was she, by making him feel too sure of her, practically throwing him into Louise's arms?

"I had this in mind, when I invited you to play golf with me tomorrow," Gary said smoothly. "I haven't been blind to the way things were going."

"You think Walter is falling in love with Louise?" Sally asked in a strained voice.

Gary smiled faintly. "I can't conceive of a man preferring Louise to you. But you are making it very easy for her, by letting Walter feel too sure of you."

Sally breathed an angry sigh. Gary's reasoning might be faulty, but she couldn't deny what she had seen tonight. Her lips set firmly. "I'd like to play golf with you tomorrow, Gary."

"Wise girl!" Gary applauded.

When Sally entered the dressing room, she found Louise seated on a divan, straightening a twisted stocking.

Louise's eyes raised quickly, and they held a triumphant light. "Still looking for Walter?" Louise asked.

Sally ignored the thrust. "I was looking for you, Louise."

Louise made the stocking snug, rose to her feet. "Well, here I am," she said challengingly.

"And feeling very proud of yourself, I suppose?"

"Very," Louise grinned.

"Was it so difficult to persuade Walter to kiss you?" Sally purred sweetly. Louise smiled but Sally saw she was stung.

"It wasn't the first time Walter has kissed me," Louise said bluntly, "nor will it be the last."

"I believe that it was the first time," Sally said quietly, "and that it will be the last."

Louise smiled faintly, shrugging. "This places Walter in rather a difficult position, doesn't it?"

"Why should it?" Sally was puzzled.

Louise laughed. "If he admits that he kissed me because he wanted to, you'll hate him. If he places the blame on me, you'll despise him."

It came to Sally suddenly that she had an adversary worthy of her steel. She realized that she had underrated the girl in the past. Realized that what Louise had said was nothing less than the truth. But she shook her head. "I shall neither hate nor despise him. It would suit you too well if I did."

"Then Walter will despise you for letting him get away with it," Louise pointed out slyly.

The truth again—and Sally suppressed a shiver. She forced her lips, which wanted so badly to tremble, into a carefree smile. "Is a kiss to be taken so seriously?" she asked, and saw that Louise didn't like this attitude.

"You'd better jilt Walter," Louise warned her in trembling tones, "before he jilts you. And while you still have Gary Neylands in love with you."

"Gary isn't concerned in this," Sally said coldly.

"Gary is very much concerned in this," Louise snapped. "I imagine Gary cut Walter's salary, simply because you refused him something he wanted."

Sally winced. *So Walter has been telling his troubles to Louise.* Somehow, this hurt worse than anything else. "Walter can conduct his business affairs without my help or yours," she retorted.

Louise's lips were twisted. "How do you think Walter will feel when he realizes that Gary hired him just to please you?"

"It isn't true," Sally said angrily.

"It's true, and you know it."

Sally's sense of the ridiculous came to her rescue then. They were not acting like two young women, but like two small girls in pinafores, squabbling over a stick of stripped candy. She turned to the door, "I shall advise Walter to kiss you every chance he gets." Sally flung a frowning glance across her shoulder. And carried with her, as she returned to the ballroom, a picture of Louise's chagrined face.

Walter came to meet her and his hang-dog look aroused a faint pity within her. She forced a smile. "Have you had enough philandering for the evening, Walter?"

"Now, Sally," he began, and swallowed painfully.

Sally tucked her hand under his arm. "I want to go home."

Walter agreed, but she could see that he wasn't pleased at the prospect of being alone with her. They were halfway home before either of them spoke again; then Sally smiled at him and kept her promise to Louise.

"I want you to kiss Louise every chance you get, Walter."

Walter's jaw hung slack. "You want me to—" But he couldn't go on with it.

Silently, Sally thanked Louise for showing her that only humor could save the situation.

"You— you're not angry?" Walter asked, bewildered.

"Do I sound angry?" Sally said lightly.

Walter agreed rather resentfully that she didn't. "Shall I explain how it happened?"

“Not unless you want me to hate or despise you,” Sally said evenly, and Walter gasped.

“I don’t understand you, Sally. I thought you would give me the devil.” His face cleared suddenly. “I understand now. You are tired tonight. We’ll discuss it in the morning.”

“I’m going to play golf with Gary in the morning. But we won’t discuss what happened tonight . . . then or ever.”

Walter gave her a frowning glance. “But you had a date to go swimming with me.”

Sally closed her eyes and her thoughts were almost prayerful. “Make him demand that I break that date with Gary. Make him threaten to beat me if I don’t.”

Walter said surlily, “I suppose I deserve this.”

Sally opened her eyes, hating herself for her weakness, excusing herself because love made you weak. “Do— do you want me to break my date with Gary?”

Walter drove silently for some moments, his scowling eyes fixed on the road ahead. Then he said resentfully, “You shouldn’t have made a date with him, Sally. But since you have, you can’t break it without making him sore at both of us.”

Sally looked away from him, shivering.

CHAPTER 19

Hard on the Mouth

Sally carried troubled thoughts with her when she went to work Monday morning. She had played golf with Gary Neylands and hadn't found it such a disagreeable task. And now, entering Ulmer's on a bright, sunny morning, she was still wondering why Walter had kept away. Was he angry because she had kept her date with Gary? Or did he, as Louise had hinted, despise her for letting him get away with it? She tried to banish these questions from her mind as she entered Philip Ulmer's office. She sank into a chair, sighing. "I've just about run out of prospects, Mr. Ulmer."

Ulmer smiled at her. "There are fifty thousand people in Avondale; and thousands of them have the bad taste to drive other makes of automobiles."

Sally recognized the truth of this, but it was too indefinite to be helpful. She smiled ruefully. "Perhaps I'd better start a house-to-house campaign."

Ulmer shook his head. "You are acquainted with most of the well-to-do people here. It should be easy for you to think of prospective buyers."

Sally realized that she had given too much thought to Walter over the weekend, and not enough to the business of disposing of Duluth automobiles. She rose to her feet frowning thoughtfully. Carruth Wade wanted to see her about a Duluth later in the week, but, even if he did buy, it would add nothing to her bank account since he was a creditor of the defunct Citizens Bank. Suddenly she remembered a woman who had been a girlhood friend of her mother's. "I believe I'll call on Mrs. Mildred Curtis," she told Ulmer. "She lives quite a distance out on Sharon Road, but she can afford a Duluth."

Ulmer nodded his agreement. "She inherited a nice income from her husband. It might be worth the long trip."

Sally's spirits lifted a little. She had decided that at least half of her sales must bring her a commission; and she was remembering that Mrs. Curtis was not one of the bank's creditors.

"Jeff might be able to give you some more prospects," Ulmer suggested.

Sally stiffened. "I can find my own prospects." The twinkle in Ulmer's eyes puzzled and irritated her.

"Do you dislike Jeff, Sally?"

"Of course not," Sally said coldly. "It's just that he—well—" And was furious because she couldn't find words with which to describe her feeling for Jeff.

"I think I understand," Ulmer said, smiling faintly. "People feel that way about Jeff at first, but most of them learn to like him very much. So you had better watch your step."

"There's no danger of that," Sally retorted, and hurried from the office. Watch her step, indeed!

~ ~ ~

Following the curving driveway, which led to the big house, Sally enumerated in her thoughts the good points of the car she drove. And then giving her name to the trim maid who answered the door, she decided to forget that line of approach. Mrs. Curtis, she reminded herself, was a family friend. The maid conducted her to a spacious living-room and a few minutes later Mrs. Curtis appeared. She was a woman of middle age, with a lined, rather petulant, face. Listening to Mrs. Curtis' cool greeting, Sally remembered that the woman had not called on her mother since the bank fiasco. Sally conveyed her mother's good wishes, and for a few moments they chatted of mutual acquaintances.

"I've been intending to call on your mother," Mrs. Curtis said in a voice that made Sally doubt it. "But my health hasn't been very good lately."

Sally expressed the proper sympathy, then decided to make known the reason for her visit. "I'm selling Duluth automobiles, Mrs. Curtis," she began, smiling, but something in the woman's widening eyes stopped her.

"You . . . Sylvester Boyce's daughter . . . selling automobiles," Mrs. Curtis said in shocked tones.

Sally nodded. "I've sold some, too," she said calmly. "I thought I might be able to sell you one."

"What can your father be thinking of to permit such a thing!" Mrs. Curtis breathed.

Sally's smile forsook her. "We have to live, you know," she said quietly.

"I can't believe that your father knows about this," Mrs. Curtis said coldly.

"My father knows and approves."

Mrs. Curtis made a mouth of distaste. "And what does your mother think about it?"

"She doesn't mind."

"I feel sure that she does," Mrs. Curtis declared.

Sally swallowed certain bitter words that begged for expressions. If you wanted to become a good salesman, you had to keep cool. "Won't you let me demonstrate the new Duluth?" she asked. "It's a grand car."

Mrs. Curtis rose to her feet, her lips compressed. "I can't encourage you in your mad course, Sally," she said firmly. "I would feel that I had betrayed your mother's confidence."

~ ~ ~

Sally was driving slowly back toward Avondale, and her thoughts buzzed like a hive of angry bees. Friends! What good were they when you were in trouble? Why, they weren't half as reliable as the engine purring under the hood.

And then the engine died—as if to give the lie to her thoughts—and the car rolled to a stop. Sally left the car, raised the hood, and glared at the engine. Then her angry eyes strayed down the road and she saw a roadside hot dog stand. She trudged hopelessly down the road. The world was conspiring to make things difficult for Sally Boyce. She would inquire, but she knew without asking that the owner of the stand would have no telephone. The man amazed her by admitting that he had a telephone and telling her that she could use it. And Sally felt a shade better as she called the repair department at Ulmer's and made known her plight. The mechanic promised to send help forthwith.

Seated in the car again, Sally settled down in a corner of the seat and tried to think of another prospective buyer for a Duluth. The sun was hot—she heard a bird singing in the adjoining woods—

A teasing voice awoke her. "So, this is the way you spend your time when out selling cars."

Sally sat upright, hoping that her ears had deceived her. But no, it was Jeff Rainey, with an irritating twinkle in his eyes. "You!" she whispered resentfully.

"Me," Jeff admitted genially, then asked, "What's wrong?"

Sally's shoulders raised. "If I knew, I wouldn't have sent for help."

Jeff laughed and stepped to his Duluth roadster, which was parked alongside her sedan. He lifted out a large can of gasoline. "Women usually run out of gas," he said cheerfully.

"But of course men never do," Sally said spitefully, and prayed that this wasn't her trouble. It would be just too awful if it were something as simple as that.

Jeff disappeared behind her car and, a moment later, she heard the tell-tale gurgling of gasoline flowing into her tank. She left the car, wondering if he was playing another trick on her. It would be just like him.

"Kick the starter," Jeff called and then he saw that she was standing beside him. "It might happen to anybody."

"There's something wrong with the engine, too," she avowed stubbornly.

"A Duluth salesman," he adjured her, grinning, "never admits that there is something wrong with a Duluth engine."

"Indeed!" was the best she could manage at the moment.

"Did you have any good luck this morning, Sally?"

"I called on an old friend of the Boyce family," she said bitterly. "I didn't sell a car."

"Don't let it get you down," Jeff sympathized. "I've been thrown out on my ear so many times I've learned to enjoy it." He frowned at her. "And now you might place your dainty foot on the starter."

Sally very definitely did not want to step on the starter, not while Jeff was here to jeer at her if the engine started. And she had an uneasy feeling that it would start. She watched him, frowning, as he replaced the cap on the gas tank.

"I think I'll stay here a little while," she told him. "I'm in no hurry to get back to town."

Jeff moved past her, set the can down, and slid into the seat of her car. He stepped on the starter and the engine purred alive. Jeff listened for a moment to the sound of the engine, then stepped to the ground again.

"Runs like a greased greyhound," he grinned.

"Go ahead and laugh!" Sally said angrily.

Jeff's face said that he was caught between amusement and something else. Something more disturbing. "You're a real cute little rascal," he said softly, "when you're mad."

Sally glared at him. "How could I know that the darn car was about out of gas?" she wailed.

Jeff was staring at her now as if he had never seen her before. Suddenly he gave a choked cry and bounded toward her, a flame in his eyes. He flung his long arms about her and her heels left the ground as he whirled her around. He set her down, kissed her hard on the mouth. "God love your little heart!" he cried deliriously. "You've given me a million-dollar idea!"

CHAPTER 20

Jeff's Invention

Sally wrenched herself free of Jeff's arms and stumbled back, while anger and fear fought for mastery in her heart. Without any warning, and for no reason at all, he had grabbed her and whirled her dizzily and had set a kiss on her mouth.

"If you ever kiss me again," Sally choked, "I'll— I'll—"

"Shut up!" Jeff commanded. "Can't you see I'm thinking?"

Sally's palm itched to contact his cheek. He had dared to kiss her, and now he dared to snap at her for objecting. But what had he meant when he said that she had given him a million-dollar idea?

Jeff ran impatient fingers through his hair, screwed up his eyes, grinned suddenly. "Yes, it's a peach of an idea!" he breathed, and then he seemed to be aware of her again. "And I owe it all to you, you cute little redheaded brat."

Redheaded brat! Sally's fingers curled—and then that killer of cats got the best of her. "What do you mean you owe it all to me? You talk as if you were crazy."

Jeff's eyes twinkled at her. "I'm crazy like a fox," he said with becoming modesty.

Sally's fingers uncurled of themselves. He looked like a small boy who had found a ticket to a World Series ball game. You couldn't slap a gleeful small boy. Jeff sat down on the running board, pulled Sally down beside him, ignoring her sputtering protest.

"Want to hear the details, Sally?"

"No!"

"Since you insist, I suppose I'll have to tell you," Jeff grinned, and became suddenly very serious and very technical. "Practically all cars have a gauge on the dash-board, or on the gas tank itself," Jeff was saying, "which shows the driver when the gas is running low. But the gauge is silent and it is easy for the driver to overlook it, just as you did this morning."

Sally thought excitedly, "It's a grand idea!" And said skeptically, "It might work."

"But with my invention," Jeff continued, just as if he hadn't heard, "there will be no chance for the driver to overlook the fact that his gasoline supply is running low. When the float in the gas tank reaches a certain level, it will make an electrical contact and a buzzer on the dash-board will sound the warning."

Sally pictured herself driving through the country, having forgotten to see to her gasoline supply. Then being warned by a sustained buzzing that she had only enough gas left to go a few miles. Yes, every car owner would want such a device!

"Just wait'll your dad hears about this," Jeff said happily. "He'll probably jump right out of bed."

"Then you'd better not tell him," Sally objected. "Jumping out of bed isn't likely to improve his condition. You'd better take your ideas to someone like Gary Neylands," she advised. "Dad can't help you."

"Can't he," Jeff said blandly. He rose to his feet, lifted her with him. His eyes fell on the hot dog stand down the road. "Just to repay you for the million-dollar idea, I'm going to buy you a hamburger, Sally. Ain't I bighearted?"

"I don't want to be critical of your manners, Mr. Rainey," she said with elaborate sarcasm, "but I do wish that you would never kiss me again."

Jeff looked at her blankly. "Did I kiss you?"

Sally glared at him. Being kissed was bad enough, but to have it forgotten so quickly was maddening. "Yes, you did!" she snapped.

Jeff's eyes were amused. "Did you enjoy it, Sally?"

Sally ignored his impudent question. "It is the height of poor manners to force your attentions on a girl who is in love with another man."

"Are you in love with somebody?"

"I'm in love with Walter Norris," she said coldly.

"Oh, you aren't in love with him," Jeff said quietly. "That's just one of those boy and girl things, known in esthetic circles as calf-love."

Sally's voice trembled with indignation. "Don't you dare say such a thing, Jeff Rainey!" Her hand drew back—

Jeff said grimly, "If you slap me, Sally Boyce, I'll shake the breath out of you."

That burning impulse left her magically. His determination was there in his eyes for her to see and to be warned. Jeff's smile blossomed out again.

"I might marry you myself, Sally . . . if I can think of it sometime when I'm not busy."

"I hate you!" she choked.

"But I haven't time to think about it now," Jeff went on, unabashed. "I'm too busy with my ideas."

It was on the tip of her tongue to order him never to come to her house again, but she remembered how much better her father looked. It might not be due to Jeff's visits, but she couldn't take the chance. Sally turned and jumped into her car, stepped on the starter, and the Duluth engine lived up to its reputation.

"What a car!" Jeff said admiringly, "and what a girl!"

Staring at him, Sally had an uneasy feeling that she had come out second best in this encounter. Surely, there must be some way by which she could have penetrated Jeff's armor and hurt him. She wanted to hurt him more than she had ever wanted anything.

"I understand that you are going to marry Carol Putnam," she began, and hesitated.

"Do you?" Jeff prompted, his eyes searching hers.

"—for her money!" Sally finished angrily. Then, seeing him grow white about the month, seeing the blazing contempt in his eyes, she regretted her words more than she had ever regretted anything. Quickly she threw the car into gear, feverishly anxious to escape his accusing stare. A mile down the road, tears flooded her eyes. "I'm hateful," she whispered. "Hateful!"

~ ~ ~

Walter came to the house that night and his complacent expression, when she met him at the door, aroused her curiosity. "Did you have a good a day, Walter?"

'Fine!" he said, and Sally felt that he was withholding some good news as they walked into the living room.

Walter sank into a chair, crossed his legs, smiled at her. "Did you have a good game of golf yesterday, Sally?"

Sally studied his face, wondering if he still felt resentful because she had played golf with Gary. But apparently, he didn't. "Good enough," she said. "I expected to see you last night."

"I was too busy," Walter said, and smiled at her again. "Gary has put me back to forty dollars a week."

"Oh, splendid!" Sally cried, then sank down in a chair as a suspicion struck her. She had refused Gary a date and Walter's Salary had dropped to twenty dollars a week. She had given Gary a date and Walter's salary had risen to forty dollars a week.

"You don't look very pleased," Walter charged.

"Oh, but I am!" Sally protested, ashamed of her suspicion. "I believe you are going to do well, Walter." Staring at his pleased face, it came to her suddenly that he was holding something back. There was something else—something even better—that he had not disclosed yet. "Tell me the rest, Walter," she urged, smiling.

Walter looked at her quickly, then just as quickly away, his brows together in a frown. "Oh, it's nothing. Nothing definite, anyway."

But Sally was badly in need of encouraging news. Even without that unpleasant episode with Jeff Rainey, it had been a heartbreaking day, a day filled with people who could not be persuaded to look at a Duluth car. "Please tell me, Walter," she begged, and realized that he was uneasy about something.

"We may be able to get married sooner than you think, darling. I'm working on a deal that may bring me several thousand dollars."

Sally stared at him. They had hoped so long—hoped until it seemed madness to continue hoping. And now he was telling her—but in an uneasy tone of voice—that they might be married sooner than they had expected. "How are you going to make the money, Walter?" she asked, and realized that her voice sounded as uneasy as his.

"There are lots of ways of making the money," he evaded.

"You mean that you don't want to tell me?" Sally asked, hurt.

She heard a car stop before the house, and, a moment later, a knock sounded on the front door. Sally knew that it was Jeff, come to see her father. Knew, as she had known all day, that she must apologize to Jeff for the terrible thing she had said to him. The memory of her hateful declaration made her shiver. "I'll be back in a moment, Walter," she said, rising, and went to answer Jeff's knock.

Jeff moved quickly through the door when she opened it. He didn't even glance at her, but strode on past.

"Jeff!" Sally called. But Jeff was taking the stairs now, three steps at a time. His broad shoulders disappeared, and Sally realized, with a sinking heart, that she had wounded him past forgiveness. Knew that his contagious smile would never be directed at her again. She felt very sober as she returned to the living room, to meet Walter's curious gaze.

"Who was that, Sally?"

"Jeff Rainey," Sally replied, in a voice that sounded strange to her own ears.

Walter stared at her silently for a moment, then he asked, "Has Jeff been having any more ideas lately, Sally?"

Sinking into a chair, Sally wondered about his sudden interest in Jeff's ideas. Heretofore he had professed contempt for both Jeff and his inventions. She recalled uneasily, that she had told Walter about Jeff's idea for a radiator and gas tank cap. She shrugged the thought away. When you loved a man, you had no secrets from him.

CHAPTER 21

Lucky Slap

Walter repeated his question, "Has Jeff been having any more ideas lately, Sally?"

Sally looked at him, thinking of the idea that had come to Jeff today—the device to protect motorists against suddenly empty gas tanks. She remembered how Jeff had grabbed her, how her heels had left the ground as he whirled her, how his lips had met hers.

"What's wrong, Sally?" Walter was asking. "You look pale."

Sally drove that outrageous picture from her thoughts and composed her face. She didn't want to think of Jeff, and so she ignored Walter's question about Jeff's latest idea. "You haven't told me how you expect to make all that money," she evaded. Walter's eyes left her face, but she felt that he was disappointed.

"To tell you the truth, it's confidential, Sally. I can't tell you about it yet."

His manner aroused her dread. "Is Gary Neylands connected with it in some way, Walter?"

Walter was staring at the floor; his brow was creased in a stubborn scowl. "Sorry, Sally. I can't explain it now."

"Don't you trust me?" she asked resentfully.

Walter's tone was just as resentful. "It seems to me that you should be satisfied that I have a chance to make some money." His face softened a little. "Are you going to be one of those wives who want their husbands to explain everything they do?"

"I'll be too busy trying to sell Duluths," Sally replied stiffly, and saw him shake his head.

"If this deal of mine goes through, it won't be necessary for you to work."

Sally felt that she should be elated by what he said, but she wasn't. Selling automobiles was heart breaking at times, but it was fascinating, as well. “I rather like selling,” she told him. “I’d like to continue with it after we are married.”

Walter’s voice showed his impatience. “That’s my principal reason for wanting to make money, so you will never have to work again.”

“But I don’t mind working,” Sally protested.

“Can’t you consider my wishes once in a while?” Walter asked angrily.

~ ~ ~

Mrs. Boyce entered the room, and Sally realized that Walter was glad of the interruption. He chatted with her mother for a few minutes, then rose and made his excuses. Sally went with him to the door, and when she returned to the living room, she saw curiosity in her mother’s eyes.

“Is Walter getting along all right, dear?”

Sally nodded. “He is still working for Gary. He expects to make a lot of money soon.”

Mrs. Boyce’s brows rose. “Walter expects to make a lot of money?” she asked in surprise.

Sally didn’t quite like her mother’s tone of surprise, and was further annoyed to recall that she had felt the same emotion. “Walter thinks we will be able to get married soon,” Sally said quietly.

Mrs. Boyce stared at her thoughtfully. “How does Walter plan to make this money, Sally?”

Sally wished now that she hadn’t mentioned the matter. She felt confused before her mother’s searching gaze. “He— he didn’t say.”

“If Walter Norris makes a lot of money,” Mrs. Boyce said bluntly, “I shall consider it nothing less than a miracle.”

Sally came quickly to his defense. “Other men make money. Is there any reason why Walter shouldn’t?”

Her mother smiled faintly, shrugged. “Some men have brown eyes, but Walter’s are grey.”

“Meaning?”

“That Walter lacks what it takes to make money.”

“You used to approve of Walter,” Sally said resentfully.

“So I did,” Mrs. Boyce acquiesced, smiling, “but we don’t know much about a man until he is broke and out of work. I still think we should accept Mr. Neylands loan and send you father to that specialist. Then I think you should break your engagement to Walter, and consider Mr. Neylands as a possible husband."

"Never," Sally said vehemently.

~ ~ ~

Sally lay long awake that night, trying to see her problems clearly, trying to find a solution for them. But when she went to work the next morning, she admitted to herself that she was no nearer to a solution. She had set herself one task to be accomplished today; she would see Jeff Rainey and apologize for her unwarranted accusation. And so, she asked about Jeff when she entered Philip Ulmer's office.

"Jeff left here a few minutes ago," Ulmer told her. "Is there something I can do for you?"

Sally shook her head. "No. It's something—well, personal." And she felt herself flushing before the twinkle in Ulmer's eyes.

"There have been two telephone calls for you this morning," Ulmer told her. "One from Adolph Gingrich; the other from Gary Neylands. Gingrich wants you to come to his place; Neylands wants you to telephone him."

Sally telephoned Gary first and felt no surprise when he asked her to have luncheon with him. Hesitating, it came to her that Gary might know something about Walter's mysterious plan to make money.

"I believe that I have another prospect for you, Sally," Gary was saying.

That decided her. "At one o'clock?" she suggested.

Gary agreed. "I'll meet you at the Gordon Hotel grill."

~ ~ ~

Parking the car in front of Gingrich's place, she wondered why he had sent for her, had something gone wrong with his Duluth? But Gingrich's beaming face, when she entered his office, drove that thought from her mind. She sat down in the chair he indicated, returning his smile.

"How is the Duluth running?" she asked.

"Swell!" Gingrich replied, then he chuckled. "I bet you're wondering why I sent for you."

Sally considered it thoughtfully, smiling. "Maybe you want to buy another Duluth?"

Gingrich shook his head, grinning. "But my brother-in-law, Heinrich Kleber, wants to buy one. He wants you to bring it to his house tonight, so his wife can see it too, He's a railway engineer."

Sally's smile trembled. She had called on many old friends of the Boyce family and few of them had seemed anxious to be of help to her. But this stranger—whose face she had slapped!—was bubbling over with happiness because he could help her.

"Heinrich isn't a creditor of your papa's bank," Gingrich continued happily, "so you will make a commission on the sale."

Sally blinked the mist away from her eyes. "I'll call on him tonight," she promised, and thanked him, and felt that life was worth living as she left. If you lost friends, through a change in fortunes, you could replace them with new and better ones.

~ ~ ~

She made a number of calls that morning. All of them were unsuccessful, but she still felt happy when she met Gary in the Hotel Gordon that noon.

Gary studied her flush face for a moment. "Something tells me that you have sold a car," he smiled.

Sally shook her head. "No. But I have a good prospect, a railway engineer."

Gary chuckled, guiding her toward the grill. "Wherever do you meet such people, Sally?"

A waiter came to meet them, so Sally didn't have to explain that this prospect had come to her as a result of slapping a man's face.

Gary smiled at her as the waiter left with their order. "Perhaps you will be too busy to call on the prospect I have for you?"

Sally denied it vigorously. "My luck hasn't been so good lately, Gary. I must sell cars this week."

"I'll do all I can to help you," Gary said seriously, and gave her the name of his prospect, a real estate broker. "He's trying to sell me a tract of land adjoining my plant." He happened to mention that he was buying a car, so I told him about you and the fine car you sell."

"You are very kind," Sally said gratefully.

Gary shrugged. "He said for you to telephone for an appointment."

Sally nodded, and then the waiter arrived with their food. While eating, Sally wondered again if she should ask him if he knew anything about Walter's plan, and again she decided against it.

"I'm very pleased with Walter's work," Gary told her presently.

Sally's heart beat a little faster. Was he going to clear up the mystery? "I'm glad that Walter is doing well," she said earnestly. "He seems to think that we will be able to be married soon." She was puzzled by the change in Gary's eyes. They had held a sparkle, but they were dully blank now and his smile didn't look genuine.

"Indeed!" Gary said quietly, and was silent for some moments. Then he looked at her and the blankness was gone from his eyes. "Are you really determined to marry him, Sally?"

It was Sally's turn to look blank. "Why, of course I am! I thought you knew that, Gary."

"I didn't," Gary said rather grimly, "and I don't."

Listening to his grim voice, Sally was reminded that several people recently had said the same thing—Louise Ives, her own mother, Jeff Rainey. "Walter and I will be married just as soon as we can," she said firmly.

Gary's voice was even firmer. "I predict that you will never marry Walter, Sally!"

CHAPTER 22

Truth Revealed

Sally stared at Gary with resentful eyes. He had been kind to her and still kinder to Walter, but he had no right to predict that she would not marry Walter.

Gary smiled faintly. “My prediction is based on my hopes, Sally.”

“I don’t understand you, Gary,” she said coldly.

“I think you do,” Gary said softly. “I think you know that I have more than a friendly feeling for you.”

It came to Sally suddenly that she did know, that she had known all along. But that she had determinedly shut her eyes to her knowledge. “Is that why you have been kind to Walter?” she asked dully, and prayed that he would answer in the negative.

“That’s why I gave Walter a job,” Gary admitted. “But it is possible that he will prove of value to me.”

“You shouldn’t have given him a job because of me,” Sally cried. “It wasn’t fair to either of us. Walter could have found a job elsewhere.”

“He wanted the job and you wanted him to have it, and so he got it,” Gary said quietly. “There’s no reason why he shouldn’t make good with me . . . if he wants to.”

But something else occupied her thoughts now. Gary loved her, had loved her all along!

“I’m a very lonely man, Sally,” Gary said gently. “Until I met you, I was content to be lonely.”

“You mustn’t say such things!” Sally protested. “I am going to marry Walter.”

“But you aren’t married to him yet,” Gary reminded her. “So there is no reason why you shouldn’t listen to me.”

“I don’t want to listen,” Sally said stiffly.

Gary leaned toward her, his face very earnest. "Haven't you felt bewildered lately, Sally? I mean about yourself and Walter . . . your feelings for each other?"

"I don't care to discuss it," Sally said angrily, and wondered disconsolately how Gary knew about her bewilderment.

"You and Walter had much in common, when both of you had money," Gary continued calmly. "But now that neither of you has money, you have nothing in common. Misfortune has changed both of you, but in a different way."

"It hasn't changed my feelings for Walter," Sally said stoutly.

"It has changed your feeling for him," Gary contradicted, "and it has changed his feeling for you." His gray eyes held her by a strange fascination. "I want you to marry me, Sally. Walter is a splendid boy," Gary said smoothly. "He will make some other girl—say Louise Ives—very happy. He'd make you wretched, Sally."

"I believe that Walter will make me happy," Sally said firmly. "Anyway, I'm willing to risk it." Suddenly she felt uneasy. "I think that Walter should know how you feel about me," she stammered. "He might not want to go on working for you."

Gary Neylands was amused. "I think that Walter has guessed my secret. In fact, I think everyone but you has guessed it."

"You think that Walter knows!" she whispered, aghast.

Gary laughed. "Walter isn't exactly blind, Sally."

"But he never said anything to me about it," she cried.

A little color stole into Gary's face; his eyes were shining. "Sooner or later, you will realize that you can't marry him, Sally. When that time comes, I shall be very happy."

Sally rose to her feet, frowning. "I want to thank you for a very delicious luncheon, Gary."

Gary was sober as he rose and placed a bill by his plate.

"You are not angry, Sally," he said with conviction. "I have given you no reason to be. I have simply made my hopes known to you, because I felt that you should know."

Walking with him toward the lobby, Sally recognized the truth of what he had said. But it made her feel no better. Gary had declared himself finally, which made it impossible for her to accept further help from him. She looked at him as she climbed into her car. She felt that she should be angry with him, but she wasn't. You couldn't be angry with a man like Gary Neylands because he had fallen in love with you.

"You must not hope, Gary," she said kindly. "It can't possibly do you any good."

"I shall go on hoping," Gary said quietly, "and I have a hunch that my hopes will materialize."

~ ~ ~

Driving back to Ulmer's, Sally felt a sense of relief. She had one thing less to wonder about. She had had an uneasy feeling all along that Gary might expect some reward for his kindnesses, and now that her suspicion had borne fruit, she felt that one of her problems had found a solution.

Entering Philips Ulmer's office, she remembered that she must see Jeff Rainey today and present her apology.

"I told Jeff you wanted to see him," Ulmer advised her when she questioned him. He looked at her curiously. "Jeff didn't say anything . . . just scowled at me."

Sally recalled Jeff's eyes as she had seen them yesterday, and shivered. Never had she seen eyes so filed with contempt. She told Ulmer that she was going to call on Heinrich Kleber that night and that she would want a freshly polished demonstrator.

"I'll see to it," Ulmer promised. "We'll be closed when you get back, but I'll have the night watchman leave the service department door open until you get in."

~ ~ ~

When Sally returned to Ulmer's late that night, she was very tired but very happy. Heinrich Kleber and his plump little wife—and even his five plump little children—had been delighted with the Duluth. And Heinrich was coming to Ulmer's at noon tomorrow to conclude the deal.

"The Boyces won't go hungry tomorrow . . . or the day after," Sally thought happily, as she maneuvered the Duluth through the big door of the service department. Bringing the car to a stop, she saw a man standing before a workbench at one side of the room. He was clad in oil-spotted coverall, and there was something familiar about the back of his head. "I'm sorry, Jeff," Sally said huskily.

Jeff scowled at the contraption and muttered something unintelligible.

"I don't know what made me say it, Jeff. I don't believe anything of the kind. Carol is a wonderful girl and I owe her an apology, too."

"Where did you get that idea?" Jeff growled.

"You made me so mad," Sally explained miserably. "It— it just popped out."

Those coverall-clad shoulders beside her were shaking, and a wave of relief swept over her. She even found it possible to join in the laughter. And vowed that never again would she allow herself to be angry with him.

"Did I really make you mad, Sally?" Jeff asked in a moment.

The old twinkle was back in his eyes and Sally found it comforting to see it there. It seemed strange to her now that she had ever thought that she hated him. Jeff had been kind to her and even kinder to her father.

"You made me furious," she admitted, and glanced up at him. "Will you forgive me?"

"Sure," Jeff said gruffly; then he grinned at her. "Shall we kiss and make up?"

Sally edged away. "We can make up without that," she said reprovingly, and changed the subject. "I want you to call on a prospect tomorrow, Jeff."

Jeff's eyes searched hers. "You want me to call on a prospect? Why don't you call on him yourself?"

"I have a reason," Sally said, and then she told him the name of the real estate broker Gary had mentioned.

"He can afford a Duluth, all right," Jeff said thoughtfully. "But I don't see why you don't sell him."

"I just don't want to," Sally said uncomfortably. She remembered something suddenly. "You didn't want to sell Carol a car."

"Who gave you the prospect?"

Sally considered this question for a moment and decided that there was no reason for secrecy. "Gary Neylands."

Comprehension dawned suddenly in Jeff's eyes. "So Gary has finally announced himself?"

"How did you know?" Sally gasped.

"It's very simple. You are not the sort who would accept favors from a man who loved you, unless you returned his love."

"Something like that," Sally admitted.

Jeff looked at her sharply. "How did Gary accept your refusal, Sally?"

She smiled a little. "Gracefully."

Jeff's face was very sober suddenly. "Don't let Gary's pretty face fool you, Sally. He's plenty smart and he knows exactly how to get what he wants."

Sally looked at him in amazement. "I didn't know that you were one of Gary's admirers."

"I admire his brains," Jeff said with a smile. "He's always gotten what he wanted, except my ideas and you. And he won't rest until he gets both."

Sally smiled at him. Jeff looked very big in the coveralls and very dirty—but rather attractively so, somehow.

"I think you'd better chase along, Sally," Jeff was saying huskily. "Every so often I get a yen to kiss you, and I feel one coming on now."

Sally stepped away, frowning. "We— we can't be friends if you talk like that, Jeff."

Jeff's eyes touched her hair, her eyes, her lips, her throat. Rose to meet her eyes again. "Do we want to be friends?" he whispered.

He was bending toward her and she was trembling. His lips were coming to meet hers, and she could only stare at him, fascinated, unable to move.

CHAPTER 23

Jeff's Scheme

Jeff's lips stopped just short of hers. He straightened suddenly, smiling rather grimly. "I'd better not kiss you again," he said softly. "Not if I want to have any thoughts left for my work."

Sally felt hot color flooding her cheeks, realizing that she had made no move to avoid his kiss. She had been gripped by a strange feeling that she could not avoid it, that his kiss was as inevitable as tomorrow's sun. They were silent for some moments, then Sally's eyes went to the workbench beside them and to the queer looking apparatus on which Jeff had been working.

"What is it?" she asked.

"It isn't anything yet," Jeff replied. "But I believe it will be valuable when I get it finished." He smiled faintly. "I'm working on the idea you gave me yesterday."

"The device to warn motorists when their gasoline is about exhausted?"

Jeff said that it was. "Your dad and I will make a lot of money out of it."

Sally's eyes went quickly to his face. "I don't understand."

Jeff smiled at her again. "I mean just what I say . . . that your father and I will make a lot of money out of it."

"But I still don't understand. Why do you visit my father, Jeff? Is it because you feel sorry for him?"

"I told you that my visits were selfish," he reminded her. "I expect to profit enormously from them."

"But Dad is sick and broke," Sally said impatiently.

"He doesn't have to remain sick and broke."

Meeting his determined gaze, Sally understood suddenly what her father had meant when he said that Jeff Rainey made anything seem possible. "You think that Dad will get well and that he will recoup his fortunes?" she whispered.

"I'm betting my future on it," Jeff said quietly. "I need your father and I believe that he needs me," Jeff continued. "He is my only chance to put my inventions on the market, and I believe that he can reestablish himself through manufacturing and marketing them."

Jeff's plan was taking shape in her mind. "You want to furnish the inventions, and have Dad furnish the money necessary to do the rest of it?"

Jeff grinned. "You catch on quickly."

"But where will he get the money? So many people here think that he defrauded them through his bank."

Jeff appeared amused about something, but he merely shrugged. "That's out of my department, Sally. It's your father's business to raise the money." His eyes twinkled at her. "You are making it easier for him."

"Me!" she whispered. "But how, Jeff?"

"By selling Duluths to creditors of the bank and waving your commissions. You are paying debts you don't owe, and people are beginning to wonder if they were right in saying that the Boyces were untrustworthy."

Sally gave a delighted gasp. "Have I really been helping Dad by doing that?"

"More than you think," Jeff said gravely.

"Why didn't you tell me before?"

"You don't seem to need much telling," Jeff smiled. "You seem to have an instinct for doing the right thing."

Sally did some quick thinking. "So that's why you refused to turn over your ideas to Gary Neylands."

Jeff nodded. "Gary has made me several offers for my patents, but I turned them down. He'd make an enormous profit out of them, and I prefer that your father and I make it."

"Then you have all your ideas patented?" Sally asked.

"All but two or three I've been working on recently. I'll get those protected when I've whipped them into marketable shape."

Sally looked at him suspiciously. "Are you sure that you haven't included Dad in your plans, simply because you are sorry for him?"

Jeff's face showed amazement and impatience. "I'm helpless without him, Sally. I know nothing whatever about promotion and finance. My only chance to make any real money out of my ideas is through your father. He's the only man I know who is capable of handling it and the only man I feel that I can trust."

"Then you don't think Gary Neylands is honest?" Sally asked thinking of Walter.

Jeff smiled a little. "I think Gary keeps within the letter of the law, Sally. But I'm confident that he would steal my ideas if he thought he could get away with it."

Sally's smile answered his. "And you don't believe that my father will steal them?"

"Your father is suffering from too much honesty now," Jeff said gravely. "He went through bankruptcy and he doesn't actually owe a dollar, but he is sick, simply because he is unable to pay his moral obligations. He'll never get well until he sees the way clear to repay every dollar to the bank's creditors."

"Then you don't think sending him to that specialist would help him?"

"It wouldn't help him, because it wouldn't remove the cause of his trouble. If we can make him feel that it is possible to pay the bank's debts, you will see a remarkable change in him."

"Dad is getting better," Sally said softly. "Even Mother admits it now."

"Have you told your father about your plan for selling Duluths to the bank's creditors?"

"No. I haven't."

"Then you must do it, Sally. It will do him more good than any amount of medicine."

~ ~ ~

When she arrived home, her mother delivered a message from Walter.

"He telephoned an hour ago," Mrs. Boyce told her. "Said he would come to see you later in the evening."

Sally was anxious to see Walter for she wanted to tell him about Jeff's plan for her father. Even now, away from Jeff's enthusiastic presence, it still seemed possible. She repeated to her mother what Jeff had told her and was surprised, when she had finished, to see that her mother did not share her elation.

"It's utterly ridiculous on the face of it," Mrs. Boyce said. "Your father is a sick man and he has no money. You must realize that it is a mad scheme, Sally."

Sally heard herself repeating Jeff's firm declaration, "He doesn't have to remain sick and broke."

Mrs. Boyce looked away from her. "Mr. Neylands was here later this afternoon. He is still anxious to lend us enough money to send Sylvester to the specialist."

"You must be mistaken, Mother," she breathed.

Mrs. Boyce looked at her, frowning. "Mr. Neylands made it very definite. He tried to force a check on me today."

"You didn't take it!" Sally asked, horrified.

Mrs. Boyce shook her head. "I didn't, but I'm afraid I'll have to accept it sooner or later. Something must be done for Sylvester very soon, and I see no other way."

"But this plan of Jeff's—" Sally began.

"It's preposterous," Mrs. Boyce finished sharply. "You are too old, dear, to believe in fairy tales."

Sally's lips set stubbornly. "It isn't a fairy tale. It's true, and I believe every word of it."

Mrs. Boyce sighed impatiently. "I have listened to your advice too long, Sally. I can't rest easy much longer, refusing help that might put your father back on his feet."

"Walter expects to make a lot of money soon," Sally reminded her, and Mrs. Boyce smiled a little.

"If Walter makes this money, I will refuse Mr. Neylands' loan," Mrs. Boyce bargained. "If Walter doesn't, then I shall be forced to accept it."

"Gary proposed to me today and I refused him," Sally said quietly. She had expected her mother to show resentment, but Mrs. Boyce merely smiled.

"Did Mr. Neylands look discouraged when you refused him, Sally?"

Sally stared at her perplexedly. "No, he didn't look discouraged," she admitted; then thoughtfully, "I wonder why?"

"Because he wants to marry you and knows that he has no real competition," Mrs. Boyce answered dryly. "Mr. Neylands knows as I know that you will never marry Walter. Walter isn't the boy you fell in love with, dear. He has changed in a rather dreadful way."

"You'll feel differently if Walter makes all that money," Sally charged angrily, but Mrs. Boyce shook her head.

"It wouldn't change my opinion of Walter if he made a million dollars," Mrs. Boyce said firmly. "But if he made even a thousand dollars, I would consider it a miracle."

Sally felt suddenly very gloomy. Had Walter really changed as her mother said? And had her love for him blinded her to the change?

Mrs. Boyce was saying gently, "I only hope that you will see Walter as he really is before you marry him . . . and not afterwards."

Sally forced a smile. "I do see him as he is . . . and I like what I see."

She heard Walter's knock at the door and went to answer it, trying to forget the wounding things her mother had said. Walter bent and kissed her and the last of her doubts disappeared. He was the same boy she had learned to love; he hadn't changed in any way. Her love for him was still a steady burning flame. When they returned to the living room, Mrs. Boyce gave Walter a rather stiff greeting, but he seemed not to notice.

"I have some excellent news for you tonight," Walter said blandly. Walter gave Mrs. Boyce a triumphant glance, then he was looking at Sally again. "I finished my deal today."

"How much did you make?" Sally asked when he hesitated.

"Only five thousand dollars," Walter said, laughing.

CHAPTER 24

Breathless and Afraid

Listening to Walter's announcement that he had made five thousand dollars, Sally heard her mother's incredulous gasp and suppressed one of her own.

"You made five thousand dollars!" she whispered, staring at him with wide eyes.

Walter nodded, but he didn't seem pleased by their amazement.

"Five thousand dollars," he said again, rolling the words on his tongue. His eyes narrowed at Sally. "Do you realize what this means?"

Mrs. Boyce asked abruptly, "Would you mind telling us how you made this money, Walter?"

Walter regarded her with chilly eyes. "It was a confidential business deal, Mrs. Boyce. I'm not at liberty to discuss it."

Sally was remembering her mother's bargain, her agreement that she would refuse Gary's loan if Walter made some money. She knew that her mother was disappointed now, since she disliked Walter so heartily.

Mrs. Boyce rose to her feet, eyes on Walter. "I shall withhold my congratulations until I learn the source of the money, Walter."

"What's the matter with her?" Walter growled.

"I don't know. I suppose it's because she is so worried about Dad."

"I don't imagine your father always explained his business affairs to her," Walter said unpleasantly.

"Mother looked afraid," Sally said, frowning puzzledly. "I wonder why?"

Walter was slow in answering and she looked at him, but his eyes avoided her.

"I can explain neither her feelings nor her actions," he replied stiffly. "I know that she doesn't like me anymore, but she might at least be civil."

"When Dad gets well, Mother will become her old self again," Sally said gently, trying to soothe his feelings. But it seemed that she reminded him of another grievance.

"Gary tells me that he called on your mother this afternoon," he said petulantly. "He renewed his offer of a loan, and Mrs. Boyce refused it."

"She did right," Sally said firmly. "We can't accept a loan from Gary."

Walter sighed impatiently. "Gary wants to lend you enough money to send your father to a doctor who will cure him. And you, for no sensible reason, refuse to accept the loan. I just can't understand it, Sally."

Sally felt an angry impulse to tell him about Gary's proposal and her refusal, and on the heels of that came a desire to tell Walter why Gary had employed him in the first place. Then he would understand why she could accept no further help from Gary. She said instead, in a controlled voice, "You will have to let Mother and me decide about that."

Walter's shoulders lifted. "If you are determined to be stubborn about it, there's nothing I can do."

She told him then about Jeff's plan for her father, expecting him to show contempt as he always did when Jeff's name was mentioned. But his face showed eagerness now.

"Has Jeff been having any more ideas lately, Sally?"

Sally laughed. "Yes. He was taken with what he called a million-dollar idea yesterday." She felt herself flushing. "I happened to be present when the idea seized him."

Walter regarded her with blank eyes. "What was his idea?"

But Sally didn't want to spend the evening talking about Jeff. "Let's talk about ourselves," she said gaily, and had a feeling that Walter would have preferred hearing about Jeff's idea.

That blankness left Walter's eyes. "This deal of mine means that we can be married, Sally. Are you prepared to set a date?"

The magic moment that comes but once to most girls, the moment when she can set a definite date for her marriage to the man she loves, the moment that leaves her a little breathless, a little afraid.

"I would suggest someday next week," Walter said, and smiled at her. "I have some more good news, darling. Your mother made me forget."

Sally's eyes were wide and starry. "I don't think I can bear any more good news," she whispered ecstatically.

Walter smiled complacently. "Gary is going to pay me a hundred a week from now on."

"A hundred dollars a week?" Sally breathed, and was speechless for a moment. Then she asked, "What kind of work will you do?"

It seemed to Sally that a shadow passed across his face, but he smiled quickly.

"I'm going to work directly under Gary," he explained. "I'll be a sort of assistant general manager."

"It— it's just too wonderful, Walter!"

Walter shrugged. "My success means something else, Sally. It means that you are through peddling automobiles."

Sally shook her head, smiling. "I can't do that, Walter. It isn't the money so much, now, but Jeff Rainey thinks it will change people's opinion of Dad if I sell cars to the bank's creditors and waive my commission."

Walter's face darkened. "What nonsense! You don't have to care any longer what people think of him."

"But we do care . . . terribly!" Sally protested. "It's more important than anything else to me."

Walter frowned. "More important than marrying me?"

"Please don't feel like that," Sally begged. "I believe that Dad would get well if he thought he could pay the bank's debts."

"And you are depending on this silly plan of Jeff's to bring that about?" Walter asked contemptuously.

"I am," Sally said simply, and Walter laughed.

"I don't want to hurt your feelings, Sally, but your father couldn't raise a dollar in this town."

Walter sounded very certain and for a moment her faith wavered. Then she remembered Jeff's enthusiasm and her shoulders squared.

"I believe that Dad can raise all the money they will need," she said quietly.

"Then why doesn't you father raise enough money to feed and clothe his own family?" Walter snapped. "Why does he allow his daughter to support him?"

"We've thought it best not to tell Dad the truth about our financial condition," Sally replied angrily.

"Then you refuse to quit selling automobiles?"

"I've explained to you why I can't quit."

"People will say that Walter Norris can't support his wife," he growled.

"You care what they think about you," she pointed out, "but not what they think about Dad."

Walter looked at his watch, rose to his feet. "I must run along. I have some more work to do tonight."

Walking with him to the door, Walter asked her again to set a date for their wedding, and Sally, deciding, wished they had not come so close to a quarrel. "Would Tuesday of next week do, Walter?"

"That'll be all right." He swallowed uncomfortably, then asked, "Would you be willing to leave Avondale, Sally?"

Sally stared at him, puzzled. "But why should we? You are getting along so well here?"

"I want to go into business for myself," he explained, "and I feel that I could do better elsewhere."

Sally knew somehow that he was evading, that he hadn't stated his real reason. "I think it would be very foolish, Walter."

He looked away from her. "We'll discuss it later."

~ ~ ~

Mounting the stairs, Sally remembered her promise to Jeff Rainey, that she would tell her father about her plan for selling Duluths. When she entered his bedroom, she found him propped up against pillows, writing on a pad of paper. She seated herself on the edge of the bed and saw that the paper held a list of names, with a figure set opposite each name.

"What are you doing, Dad?"

Mr. Boyce looked thoughtful, sighed. "Kidding myself, I imagine."

"Kidding yourself about what?" she smiled.

He laid the paper down. “I’m trying to make myself believe that I can raise two hundred thousand dollars.”

“That’s a lot of money!” she murmured.

Sylvester Boyce nodded. “That young idiot Jeff Rainey actually seems to believe that I can raise that much money.” He laughed ruefully. “When he’s here, I believe it, too.”

Sally could understand that. When Jeff's eyes, shining with enthusiasm, were fixed on you, anything was possible. But $200,000 sounded like something out of a dream. Surely, Jeff didn’t believe that her father could raise it.

“Will it take that much money?” she asked.

Mr. Boyce sighed helplessly. “I haven’t checked his figures carefully yet, but I’m afraid that it will.” Mr. Boyce looked at her curiously. “Did Jeff tell you all about it?”

Sally smiled at him. “Jeff says that he is betting his future on you.” His brightening face made her add something else, “I believe that you and Jeff can put it across, Dad.”

“You’re as crazy as Jeff,” Mr. Boyce whispered, his lips twitching. He shook his head, frowning. “I can’t bear to disappoint Jeff, Sally. He hasn’t the faintest doubt but what I will raise every dollar we need.”

“And neither have I,” Sally said quietly, and found that she almost meant it.

“Since you two young idiots think I can, I suppose I’ll have to try,” he growled.

CHAPTER 25

Too Weak?

Listening to her father's growling declaration, Sally felt choked. This was the first time since his bank failed that he had shown an active interest in anything. He wasn't optimistic about raising the $200,000 needed to finance Jeff's scheme. But he had declared that he would try, and that list of names and figures on the bed showed that his brain was already busy with the problem. She asked him for the names of some of the bank's biggest creditors, and jotted them down on a piece of paper as he searched his memory.

"I'm going to spend half my time calling on them," she explained, when he was done. Her voice trembled with excitement. "We'll show Avondale that the Boyces aren't whipped!"

Mr. Boyce stared at her as if he were unwillingly gripped by her enthusiasm.

"Will we?" he asked doubtfully.

Sally drew her brows into a threatening scowl. "Don't let me catch you doubting it, young man!"

Mr. Boyce looked away from her, his lips trembling. "I'm afraid I haven't met my reverses very bravely. I didn't mind losing the money, but losing the confidence of the people of Avondale seemed more than I could bear."

"This plan of Jeff's will make it possible for you to pay off the bank's creditors," Sally said happily. "It may take several years, but that doesn't matter."

"If I could really believe that," Sylvester Boyce said wistfully, "I could leave my bed this instant."

Listening to his voice, in which hope and despair struggled for mastery, Sally was more convinced than ever that Jeff had been right about him. Despair had put Sylvester Boyce where he was and only hope could restore him to normal.

She heard a knock at the door, heard her mother answer it; then footsteps were taking the stairs, three at a time, and her father's flush face confirmed her suspicion that Jeff was about to burst upon them.

Mr. Boyce's voice sounded excited as he called to Jeff to enter.

Jeff spread a curious glance between them. "Council of war, Dad?" he asked Mr. Boyce.

"Something of the kind, Son," Mr. Boyce smiled.

Dad? Son? Sally divided a puzzled glance between them. Yesterday she would have resented this familiarity on Jeff's part, but tonight it seemed natural enough.

Jeff straddled a chair, his arms crossed on its back. "I've been whipping my latest idea into shape," he told Sylvester Boyce. "Looks like it's going to be a money-maker."

"Is that the device for warning the motorist when he is about to run out of gas?" Mr. Boyce asked.

Jeff nodded, smiling. "The one we have to thank Sally for." And then he explained how the idea had come to him.

Sally found it very pleasant to have her father and Jeff approving of her.

"Sally has some very good ideas," Jeff said, and added hastily, "and some very poor ones."

Sally thought that she was entitled to be angry, but she wasn't and it puzzled her.

"I've been studying the financial end of it, Jeff," Mr. Boyce said, and frowned. "Frankly, I can't see any possibility of raising the money."

"You could raise twice that amount by tomorrow night," Jeff said calmly. "That's why I've decided that two hundred thousand isn't enough. We might as well start right, with all the equipment we need, so I want you to raise three hundred thousand dollars."

Sylvester Boyce slumped against his pillows, sighing gustily. He gave Sally a humorously despairing glance. "You can see what I'm up against, Sally."

Sally stared blankly at Jeff. He had given her father the impossible task of raising $200,000. And now, quite calmly, he raised the amount to $300,000. She was suddenly stricken by doubt. "How much money have you, Jeff?" she asked weakly.

Jeff stared thoughtfully at the ceiling, his lips moving as he estimated his goods. "Fifty-nine dollars and sixty-five cents," he announced finally, grinning at her. "And how much have you?"

Sally told him and found that she was not very proud of her bank account now. It seemed such a pitifully small sum compared with what they needed. "What do you do with all your money, Jeff?" she asked. "You sell so many Duluths."

"It costs money to protect ideas," Jeff explained. "I spend all I make on patents."

This was understandable, Sally thought worriedly. But it didn't furnish a means for raising the huge sum he had mentioned so blithely.

"I had another idea on my way here tonight," Jeff said. He winked at Mr. Boyce, then looked at Sally again. "It's an apparatus for parking a car when the parking space at the curb isn't long enough for the usual seesaw method."

"Tell us about it," Sally ordered, and wondered why he winked at her father again.

Jeff stared at the ceiling as he explained the idea: a set of wheels suspended on hydraulic supports under the car's chassis. When you came to a short parking space, just wide enough for the car, you pressed a button and these wheels dropped to the ground, lifting the car. You pressed another button and the car slid into the parking space—sideways!

"If your car is equipped with this device," Jeff assured her blandly, "you need never again bend your fenders while trying to seesaw into a too-narrow parking space."

Sally gasped delightedly. She had suffered damaged fenders several times under those conditions. "I think it's wonderful!" she cried, and turned to her father. "Don't you agree with me, Dad?"

Sylvester Boyce refused to commit himself, but his eyes held a look of amused suspicion. "Jeff has charge of the idea department," he told Sally. "All I have to do is raise a mere three hundred thousand dollars."

Sally turned to Jeff again. She was trembling with excitement and resented his calm face. "You aren't showing your usual enthusiasm," she charged.

"Oh, I get so many million-dollar ideas," Jeff murmured, and yawned modestly.

Sally laughed. Jeff Rainey might be as preposterous as her mother and Gary and Walter said, but she found it thrilling to share in it.

"Couldn't we get along on less than three hundred thousand dollars?" Mr. Boyce asked Jeff.

Jeff turned a pair of surprised blue eyes on him. "But why should we, Dad? You can easily raise it, and you know that most young businesses fail because of improper financing."

"If I just wasn't confined to my bed," Mr. Boyce sighed.

"How do you know that you are?" Jeff asked.

Mr. Boyce stared at him with blank surprise for a long moment. Then he growled, "Why, Dr. Frobisher ordered me to remain in bed. He says I'm too weak to walk."

"Have you tried to walk?" Jeff inquired politely.

"Dad!" Sally cried, but she was too late.

Sylvester Boyce had swung his pajama-clad legs over the side of the bed. He stood erect, teetering on his shaky knees. He took a step and then another, while a look of amazement spread over his face. When he reached the hall door, he turned and slowly retraced his steps. He sank down on the edge of the bed.

"Well, I'll be!"

"Exactly," Jeff said, grinning.

"Why, Dad! You walked," Sally choked, and the expression on his face brought tears to her eyes.

Mr. Boyce looked at Jeff. "Did I walk to the door and back . . . or am I dreaming?"

"You did," Jeff said matter-of-factly, "but it's nothing to brag about."

Sally glared at Jeff. Didn't he recognize a miracle when he saw one?

Jeff met her gaze calmly. "Your father can raise that money just as easily as he walked to the door and back."

His mention of the money reminded Sally that she had some news for them. "Walter made five thousand dollars today," she said proudly.

"Five thousand dollars!" Mr. Boyce exclaimed. Then his smile teased her. "Are you sure it wasn't five million?"

Jeff Rainey asked quietly, "How did he make it, Sally?"

Sally saw that Jeff wasn't incredulous but merely curious.

"I— I don't know," she confessed.

"I'm glad to hear he is doing so well." Jeff said politely.

There was something in Jeff's eyes that made her feel uneasy, and so she looked at her father again.

"I am going to be married next week, Dad."

Jeff said quietly, "Impossible! I'll be too busy next week."

Sally looked at him. "Too busy to come to my wedding?"

"Too busy to marry you," Jeff said gravely.

Sally started to laugh; Jeff was always teasing. Her laughter died in her throat as she searched his eyes. There was no humor in them. But there was another emotion there, one that puzzled and stirred her. Only by an effort was she able to tear her eyes away from his, and look at her father again. "Walter's success makes it possible for us to be married at once, Dad."

Sylvester Boyce didn't show the expected enthusiasm. His narrowed eyes looked vaguely troubled. "I had supposed that you would get over that idea, Sally." Then he asked, "Are you sure that you want to marry Walter?"

"Of course I'm sure," Sally said quickly, firmly.

"You must remember that marriage is a serious business," Mr. Boyce said uneasily. "I'm not convinced that Walter will make you happy, dear."

Jeff Rainey cut in smoothly. "Don't let it worry you, Dad. Sally isn't going to marry Walter next week . . . or at any other time."

CHAPTER 26

A Good Reputation

When Sally reached Ulmer's the next morning, she telephoned Carruth Wade's office, asking for an appointment to show him a Duluth.

"You may see him at eleven o'clock," his secretary informed her, after consulting with Wade. "But please be here on time, as Mr. Wade is very busy."

Jeff Rainey lounged into the office, and Sally gave him a rather stiff greeting. His outrageous remarks of last night still rankled.

"Sally is going to beard the lion in his den this morning," Ulmer told Jeff. "None other than Carruth Wade."

Jeff whistled. "Going after big game, eh?" He turned to Ulmer, looking rather disconsolate. "I have no prospects for today except one that Sally gave me last night."

Ulmer laughed. "Looks like you're slipping, Jeff. A week ago you were helping Sally."

Sally found that Jeff was looking at her with a thoughtful expression in his eyes.

"Carruth Wade is one of the richest men in the state," he said blandly.

Sally felt that his remark had some hidden meaning, but she couldn't decipher it.

"Then I can accept his check?" she asked dryly.

"If you can get it," Ulmer commented, chuckling.

Jeff moved toward the door. "I want to see my prospect before his breakfast begins to disagree with him." At the door, he turned and glanced at Sally. "It's very foolish to prepare for something that isn't going to take place."

Sally entered Carruth Wade's office at ten minutes of eleven; and his secretary, a middle-aged, prim-looking woman nodded approvingly.

"You are ten minutes early, Miss Boyce."

Sally seated herself in a chair across the room and thought with pleasure of the Duluth parked in the street below. Ulmer's service department had put it in tip-top condition both inside and out.

"Good morning, Mr. Neylands!"

The secretary's greeting turned Sally's eyes to the corridor door. Gary Neylands stood there, and his eyes came to meet hers. He nodded briefly to the secretary, then moved toward Sally.

"Your appointment is for ten minutes after eleven," the secretary called after him.

Sally's heart sank. This meant that Mr. Wade was allowing her only ten minutes and she couldn't conclude her deal with him in that brief time.

Gary smiled as he sank into a chair beside her. "Are you trying to float a loan too, Sally?"

Float a loan! Sally was remembering Jeff's remark that Carruth Wade was one of the richest men in the state. This, connected with Gary's words, took on a meaning suddenly. "I came to sell Mr. Wade a Duluth," she told Gary.

"I imagine he can afford one," Gary said humorously.

Sally hardly heard him. It would be wonderful, she thought excitedly, if she could interest Carruth Wade in Jeff's scheme. Why, he alone could finance it!

"Walter tells me that you and he are planning to be married next week," Gary was saying. "Is it true, Sally?"

Sally made it more definite. "Yes. Next Tuesday."

"Will I receive an invitation?" Gary asked lightly.

"Of course," Sally replied, and wondered suddenly if Gary was the source of Walter's mysterious five thousand dollars.

"Shouldn't you be shopping for your trousseau?"

"That won't take long," Sally told him. "I can't afford a very elaborate one."

"I suppose you'll quit selling cars?"

Sally shook her head. "I can't afford to do that yet."

Gary showed surprise. "But I'm paying Walter a hundred a week, Sally. And I'm optimistic about his future."

"I have another reason for selling Duluths."

Comprehension dawned in his eyes. “Yes, I remember now.” He smiled a little. “Are your father and Jeff going ahead with their plan?”

Sally didn’t quite like his smile. “I believe that they will be successful,” she said firmly.

Gary’s smile broadened. “How much money have they raised so far?”

Sally felt color stealing into her cheeks. “You will have to ask them,” she said stiffly.

Gary’s voice was suddenly gentle. “Don’t let it worry you, Sally. When this ridiculous plan of Jeff’s falls through, I’ll see that your father is taken care of.”

“I’m afraid you underestimate my father . . . and Jeff, too,” she said coolly.

Gary shook his head, smiling. “You must remember that I talked with Dr. Frobisher about your father. He is convinced that Mr. Boyce will never leave his bed unless he is taken to that specialist.”

Sally felt like laughing. What had happened last night proved Dr. Frobisher mistaken. Then her spirits fell. Walking to the door and back didn’t mean that her father was cured, didn’t mean that he could raise the extravagant sum Jeff Rainey wanted. “Are you trying to sell Mr. Wade some auto accessories?” she asked.

Gary looked very sure of himself. “I’m going to allow Wade to lend me enough money to build an extension to my plant.”

“Mr. Wade will see you now, Miss Boyce,” the secretary called.

Carruth Wade greeted Sally cordially, waved her to a seat. “What did you want to see me about?” he asked, smiling.

Sally’s spirits fell to zero. Had he forgotten their talk at the country club? “You told me I could demonstrate a Duluth—” she began, but Wade cut her off.

“I remember now.”

“I have a Duluth parked in the front of the building. It won’t take long to show you what a wonderful car it is.”

“What’s the price of the sedan?” Wade asked.

Sally told him. “Less my commission, of course, since you were a creditor of Dad’s bank.”

Wade smiled faintly. “You make it sound very attractive. But I haven’t time to look at the car today.”

Sally's throat tightened. She remembered how cock-sure she had been in Philip Ulmer's office. She could picture the twinkle in Ulmer's eyes when she told him that she had failed. She could hear Jeff's teasing laughter. Her lips tightened suddenly. She opened her bag and removed the bill-of-sale Ulmer had given her. "Here is the bill-of-sale," she said quietly. "It isn't necessary for you look at the car." She laid the document on the desk before him; she met his surprised gaze squarely.

"You expect me to buy the car without even looking at it?" he murmured. "But how do I know that it is a good car?"

"The Duluths and the Boyces have an excellent reputation," Sally informed him, and shivered as she remembered how much money Wade had lost in her father's bank.

Carruth Wade sank back in his chair, looking more bewildered than angry. "The Duluth does have a good reputation," he admitted thoughtfully.

"And the Boyces have one equally as good," Sally declared.

Wade frowned at her. "There are people in Avondale who wouldn't agree with you."

"They will all agree with me eventually," Sally said firmly.

"You have set yourself a sizeable task," Wade warned her. "And your father is too sick to help you."

He pressed a button on his desk, and Sally's spirits fell to sub-zero. She had failed.

Wade's secretary appeared in the door. "Yes, Mr. Wade?"

Wade told the woman to make out a check to Ulmer Motor Sales Company in the amount Sally had named.

Sally's thoughts were spinning and her hand was trembling as she made out a check for the amount of her commission. Handing it to him, she saw the twinkle in his eyes and was encouraged to try her unbelievable luck still further.

"Have the sedan delivered to my residence," Wade told her.

Sally nodded. "I want to talk to you about something else, Mr. Wade."

His look wasn't encouraging; his voice was chilly. "I'm a very busy man."

"And I'm a busy girl." Her smile was shaky. "But this is something very important." And then she poured out the details of

Jeff's scheme, stuttering at times in her eagerness to get it all told. "Jeff's ideas are marvelous, and Dad is getting better every day!" she finished.

"Jeff Rainey," Wade repeated, frowning. "I've never heard of him." He looked at her sharply. "You're in love with this Jeff Rainey, aren't you?"

Sally stared at him blankly. "Why— why, of course I'm not!" she gasped.

"You sounded like it," Wade told her; then his eyes turned cold. "I don't know anything about this young man or his ideas; and your father is in no condition to do business. So I shan't be interested in the proposition. Good day, Miss Boyce."

Sally carried a heavy heart out of his office. She had dreamed a big dream and it had collapsed about her. Gary Neylands put a hand on her arm, and she came to a stop, fighting the tears.

"You must abandon your plan to marry Walter," Gary said quietly.

That firm voice made her forget her defeat. "What do you mean, Gary?"

"That you must not set your heart on marrying Walter."

"You must be mad!"

Gary's eyes were gentle, but his jaw was set. "You shall not marry him, Sally!"

Sally smiled a little as she watched him enter Wade's private office. She was remembering that Walter had five thousand dollars now, which made them independent of Gary Neylands.

CHAPTER 27

Almost Always Serious

Sally was in a sultry humor as she left the building, which housed Carruth Wade's office. She had had such high hopes of enlisting his aid in putting across the scheme that Jeff Rainey had conceived, and in which her father hoped to participate. Standing on the sidewalk, undecided where to go next, Sally decided that men were obtuse creatures. Just because she had shown enthusiasm for Jeff's ideas, Carruth Wade—*Darn him!*—had assumed that she was in love with Jeff.

Her eyes went to the highly polished Duluth parked at the curb and she thought of Carruth Wade's check in her purse. But it only reminded her of his assertion that her father was in no condition to do business, and his blunt refusal to interest himself in Jeff's scheme. Sally heaved a dismal sigh. Wade might be right about her father. Her mother had the same opinion, and so had Gary and Walter and Dr. Frobisher. Only Jeff Rainey, that mad young man, scoffed at the idea that Sylvester Boyce was a has-been.

Frowning thoughtfully, Sally walked to a corner drugstore and telephoned Dr. Frobisher's office. His receptionist told her that the doctor was preparing to go to lunch, but that he would see Sally for a few minutes if she would come to his office immediately.

~ ~ ~

Dr. Frobisher permitted himself a grave smile. "I suppose you have come to see me about your father, Sally?"

Sally nodded and put the question bluntly, "Do you believe that Dad is going to recover?"

"I see no reason why he shouldn't, given plenty of time and, of course, the proper treatment."

"What is wrong with Dad?" Sally asked, feeling that her frank questions were out of place in this urbane atmosphere.

"He's suffering from a nervous breakdown."

"What caused it, Doctor?"

His face showed impatience. "Shock."

"Dad didn't mind so much losing the money. But he was dreadfully hurt by the fact that he couldn't pay off all the creditors of the bank."

"The result is the same, whatever the cause," Dr. Frobisher said coldly.

"Are you sure of your diagnosis?" she asked.

Dr. Frobisher's beard quivered. "I am quite sure," he said stiffly.

"Then why do you advise sending Dad to that specialist?" Sally asked quickly.

"I don't feel called upon to explain my reasons for this," he said condescendingly. "I can only repeat that you should take your father to the specialist and then south for the winter."

Sally stared at him thoughtfully, then shook her head. "Even if we followed your advice, Dad would still worry about the creditors of the bank. The cause of his illness would still exist, so I don't see how it could possibly do him any good."

Dr. Frobisher pressed a button on his desk, fixed her with a blankly reproving stare. "I have neither the time nor the desire to discuss this further. I can only tell you that your father will never leave his bed unless my instructions are carried out."

Sally moved to the door, turned there. "My father left his bed last night and went for a walk, Dr. Frobisher."

His face went from pink to red. "Went for a walk? Impossible!"

"Dad walked to the hall door and back to his bed last night," Sally said, smiling. "And he felt no ill effects this morning."

"Who told him to do this!" Dr. Frobisher demanded angrily.

Sally grinned at him. "Dr. Jefferson Rainey." She closed the door, cutting off his bewildered gasp.

~ ~ ~

Eating a hurried lunch at a drugstore fountain, Sally decided that she had a crow to pick with Jeff Rainey. His veiled suggestion to her this morning—that Carruth Wade was one of the richest men in the state—had led her to try to interest Wade in Jeff's scheme. And her visit to Dr. Frobisher, from which she had learned nothing new, might be blamed on Jeff too, she thought irritably.

She found Jeff, thirty minutes later, in Philip Ulmer's office, concluding the sale of a Duluth to a man who was a stranger to her.

The man left and Jeff turned to her, his eyes blank. "Could I interest you in buying a Duluth, lady?" he inquired politely.

Sally frowned at him. "Aren't you ever serious?" she sighed.

"I have my serious moments," Jeff allowed, smiling. He nodded toward the door through which the stranger had just gone. "That was the real estate broker Gary Neylands wanted you to sell."

Sally wondered what Gary would say when he learned that Jeff, not herself, had made that sale? And decided that she would never know it if he felt resentment. Yes, Gary Neylands was clever at concealing his emotions.

She asked, "What did you mean this morning when you said that Carruth Wade was one of the richest men in the state?"

"Did you sell him a Duluth?" Jeff evaded.

"I did . . . but that isn't answering my question."

Jeff looked past her, frowning slightly. "I thought you might like to explain my scheme to him, Sally. You see, Wade isn't interested in promotion and manufacturing, but merely in financing."

"I did explain it to him."

"What did Wade say?"

"That Dad was in no condition to do business, which happens to be the truth," she replied fretfully.

"It's a debatable point," Jeff said thoughtfully. "Your father hasn't attempted to do business lately, so we can't be sure about it. Did Wade say anything else?"

Sally colored as she remembered one thing Wade had said. She frowned at Jeff. "That he had never heard of you or your ideas," she said coldly.

"But he has heard of both now," Jeff pointed out blandly. "Anything else?"

"That he wouldn't be interested in the plan."

"Perhaps you didn't explain it properly," Jeff suggested.

"I had only a minute," Sally said resentfully. "Gary Neylands was there waiting to see him."

Jeff looked pleased. "I had heard that Gary was unable to raise any more money at the banks."

"That doesn't help us," Sally reminded him.

"When we get our plant going, Gary will be one of our competitors." Jeff's eyes twinkled. "We must spend some time each day wishing bad fortune to our competitors."

Sally envied him his quiet assurance that his scheme would go through. "I called on Dr. Frobisher, too," she told him, and smiled wryly. "He is of the same opinion, still."

"Your father will never get well until he believes it is possible to pay the bank's debits." Jeff raised his brows at her. "How many times do I have to tell you this?"

Sally agreed with him in her thoughts, but his teasing manner made it impossible to admit it openly.

Jeff said quietly, "I think you have done a good morning's work, child. I find it possible to approve of you."

"Oh, you do!" she said indignantly.

Jeff nodded. "I didn't expect you to come away from Wade's office with his check for three hundred thousand dollars. I merely wanted you to give him something to think about."

"I feel confident that he isn't thinking about it," Sally said dispiritedly.

"Carruth Wade has grown rich through financing other men's ideas, Sally. He will spend at least a few minutes wondering if my ideas are worth his attention."

"And then he will forget all about it," Sally sighed.

"Until your father walks into his office, someday soon, and calls it to his attention again."

Sally had to laugh. Jeff sounded so sure, almost as if he were speaking of something that had already happened. "What if Mr. Wade decided against it?" she asked.

"Wade has never been known to turn down a good proposition," Jeff told her. "But if he does, in this case, well, there are plenty of others who will be interested."

The telephone range and Sally answered it and heard Carol Putnam's voice, congratulating her on her approaching marriage. And asking if she, Carol, might be the first to give a party for the bride-to-be? Sally thanked her and said that she might, and asked where Carol had learned about it. Carol told her that she had met Mrs. Boyce while shopping.

Hanging up the receiver, Sally smiled at Jeff. "Carol is a sweet girl. She wants to give a party for me."

"But why should she give a party for you?" Jeff inquired.

"Because I am to be married Tuesday of next week."

"I'll be too busy next week to marry you," Jeff protested.

Sally laughed. "Never serious."

"Almost always serious," Jeff insisted.

"Do you actually think that I will jilt Walter between now and next Tuesday?" she asked lightly.

"I am sure of it," Jeff said gravely. "Just as sure of it as I am that your father left his bedroom this morning and walked down stairs."

Sally stared at him. "What makes you think that my father did such a foolish thing?"

Jeff smiled. "Isn't it natural that he should try? After what took place last night, he will be curious to know just how far he can walk."

The telephone jangled again and Sally answered it. Her mother's excited voice rang in her ear. "Your father is becoming positively unmanageable, Sally! He's been tramping around upstairs all morning, and a few minutes ago he came down here demanding a big luncheon."

"I want you to come home at once. Perhaps you can do something with him."

"Let me speak him, Mother," Sally said, glaring at Jeff over the instrument. "I'll tell him to go back to bed."

CHAPTER 28

Tear-filled Eyes

Sally felt uneasy when she reached home that night. Her telephone conversation with her father that noon had not resulted satisfactorily. Mr. Boyce had told her sharply that he was through being bossed around by two women and a namby-pamby doctor. That he would in the future do exactly as he pleased without consulting anyone.

Sally hadn't told Jeff that his prediction had come true, or about her father's declaration of independence. And she was dreading the time when Jeff should learn about it, for she knew that he would laugh. She found her mother in the living room, sewing.

"How is Dad tonight?" Sally asked anxiously.

Mrs. Boyce laid her sewing down, sighed. "I really don't know," she replied helplessly. "Dr. Frobisher was here this afternoon, but he won't be here again."

Sally's voice trembled. "Why?"

Mrs. Boyce frowned worriedly. "Your father told him that he was sick of the sight of him."

Sally said quietly, "I believe that Dad is getting better. Perhaps he will be well enough to attend my wedding." She had hoped that mention of her marriage would cheer her mother, but it had the opposite effect.

"I can't bear to think of your marrying Walter!" Mrs. Boyce cried. "I know that you will be unhappy."

Staring at her mother's tear-filled eyes, Sally was prey to certain confusing thoughts. Did happiness necessarily follow marrying the man you loved? Do I really love Walter? Or have I just gotten into the habit if thinking I do? Resolutely, she shut her mind to these disloyal thoughts. You had to follow your heart, no matter where it might lead.

Mrs. Boyce rose from the chair. "I'll get supper, dear. I want you to see your father. Perhaps you will be able to do something with him."

Sally dreaded seeing him tonight. She was sure that she would find him lying on the bed, white with fatigue from his efforts of the day. And looking more hopeless than ever, having found that his strength was unequal to the task he had set for himself. She took the stairs very slowly, trying to drive her fear from her heart. No matter how exhausted and hopeless he might be, she must present a cheerful countenance, must encourage him in a voice firm with her belief in him.

She rapped on his bedroom door and waited for his quavering invitation to enter. Only silence greeted her and she leaned against the door, listening to the frightened thudding of her heart. Was he asleep, or—? She flung the door open.

"Can't a man have any privacy in his own home!" Sylvester Boyce bawled at her.

Sally's bewildered eyes found him at a table by a window. He was wearing trousers and a shirt, open at the neck. His face bore an impatient scowl. She moved on unsteady legs into the room, feeling a hysterical desire to laugh. She had been so sure that he had collapsed from his exertions of the day. Her smile trembled along with her voice. "What are you doing, Dad?"

"I suppose I'll have to rent an office downtown," Mr. Boyce growled. "It seems that I can't work here without being disturbed."

Sally remembered that he had always been amiable when he was well—unless you disturbed him while he was at work. She swallowed a lump in her throat. "You must go back to bed, Dad," she said gently. "You've done enough for one day."

But Sylvester Boyce was staring at the paper before him on the table. "Jeff's estimates are faulty," he growled. "Three hundred thousand dollars won't be enough. We must have a substantial reserve fund." He shot a scowling glance at Sally, which dared her to deny it.

She put a hand on his shoulder, smiling down at him. "Of course it's necessary," she agreed softly. No, the amount didn't matter, since he couldn't raise it anyway.

He looked up at her, a twinkle in his eyes. "I bet Jeff will be surprised when he learns that I've been up most of the day."

Sally thought disapprovingly of Jeff, who was not even surprised by miracles. "Jeff predicted that you would," she told her father.

"Oh, he did, did he?" Mr. Boyce smiled a little. Then he narrowed his eyes at her. "Why don't you marry Jeff? We need a smart boy like him in the family."

Sally frowned at him." Have you forgotten that I'm to marry Walter next week?"

Mr. Boyce shrugged, smiling. "Jeff told me that I didn't need to worry about that."

"Has it ever occurred to you that your precious Jeff Rainey might be wrong about something?" she asked stiffly.

"It never has," Mr. Boyce confessed quietly.

~ ~ ~

Bathing and dressing and eating supper, Sally's thoughts were moody. So much opposition, she considered fretfully, was enough to drive a girl into marriage, even if she didn't love the man. But this didn't mean, of course, that she wasn't in love with Walter. She was comforted later in the evening—meeting Walter at the front door—to find that her heart beat faster at seeing him. Seated beside him on the sofa in the living room, with his arm about her, she told him everything that had happened during the day.

"It's mighty nice of Carol to give a party for us," he said and then he frowned. "You must persuade your father to listen to Dr. Frobisher, Sally. If he doesn't there's no telling what may happened to him."

"But Dad wasn't getting any better while Dr. Frobisher was treating him," Sally protested.

"It might be a good idea for me to speak to your father," Walter suggested.

Sally shook her head. "Dad is in a very bad humor today, Walter. You can talk to him some other time."

But Walter rose to his feet, a determined light in his frowning eyes. "It's time that I had a talk with your father, Sally," he said decisively. "Since we are to be married so soon, I feel that I have a right to advise him."

Sally marveled at the change in Walter. A week ago, he had been gloomily uncertain of himself. Today, with five thousand dollars in the bank, he was like a new man.

"You'd better not see him tonight, Walter," she cautioned him. "He's had a very tiring day."

But Walter was moving toward the front hall and the stairs, his shoulders squared, and Sally sank back, praying that her father had vented his irritation on the doctor, her mother, and herself. She heard Walter's knock on her father's bedroom door and Mr. Boyce's answering voice was neither so loud nor so angry as she had expected. But it grew steadily louder and angrier as the moments passed, telling her that her father neither wanted nor respected Walter's advice. A slamming door muffled that angry voice, and she was caught between laughter and tears as she listened to Walter's footsteps descending the stairs.

Walter's face held a look of furious bewilderment as he appeared again in the living room. "Dr. Frobisher was right," he snarled. "Your father is losing his mind."

Sally pulled him down beside her on the sofa. "What did Dad say to you?" she asked in a muffled voice.

"Things I don't wish to repeat to a lady," Walter said stiffly.

"Dad has been cross with everybody today," Sally said persuasively. "You mustn't take it to heart."

"I'm not accustomed to being talked to in that manner," Walter said angrily. "He'd better keep a civil tongue in his head in the future. He isn't a rich banker any longer."

Sally couldn't quite manage to like this. "Dad will be as successful as ever before long," she declared.

"You'll forgive me if I doubt it," Walter said coldly. "Did you tell him about the money I made?"

Sally said that she had, and then remembering Mr. Boyce's comment, spoke quickly of her sale to Carruth Wade.

"What did your father say?" Walter persisted.

"He— he didn't say much of anything," Sally stammered, and remembering Mr. Boyce's derisive reference to five thousand dollars, "I saw Gary Neylands today in Mr. Wade's office."

"Your father is jealous of my success," Walter growled.

"Dad is jealous of no one," Sally said quietly, and found those same disturbing thoughts moving through her mind again. Is this the same man I learned to love? Is it possible that my love is nothing more than a habit? She smothered the treasonable thoughts, managed a smile. "Did you get along all right today, Walter?"

Walter admitted that he had gotten along extremely well. "I expect to be practically running the plant before long."

Sally clapped her hands, laughing delightedly. "Our luck has certainly changed for the better," she cried.

"I doubt if I will remain at the plant very long," Walter said quickly. "I am considering other plans, which may make it necessary for us to leave Avondale."

"But you are doing so well here," Sally protested.

"I believe that I would do even better elsewhere," Walter told her. "Has Jeff Rainey been visiting your father recently?"

"He was here last night."

"Has Jeff been having any more of those funny ideas of his?" Walter laughed.

Sally was angry and wondered at it, wondered why she took such pride in Jeff's ideas, wondered why she always felt called upon to defend them. "I wouldn't call them funny ideas," she said coldly. "Jeff thought of one last night that seemed wonderful to me."

"But you don't know much about such things," Walter teased.

"Just listen to this," she said proudly, and proceeded to tell him about Jeff's device for parking cars in a too-short parking space. She repeated every detail that Jeff had told her father and herself, but when she had finished the look in Walter's eyes made her feel uneasy.

"You mustn't tell anyone about this, Walter," she adjured him.

That rapt look left his eyes, his lips curled.

"It isn't worth telling," he sneered.

CHAPTER 29

Her Lips Melt

The Putnams were one of the few families in Avondale who could afford an orchestra when they gave a party; and their drawing room was probably the only one large enough to hold the crowd now gathered to celebrate Sally Boyce's approaching marriage.

Dancing with Walter, Sally wondered why she felt confused instead of happy. She had bought a lovely trousseau, and all arrangements had been made for her marriage to the man she loved. She was in his arms, dancing to pulse-stirring music. Her moody eyes passed over the crowd collected in her honor. She saw Louise Ives dancing with a young attorney. Louise's eyes came to meet hers and Sally shivered, for there was something close to hatred in Louise's expression. Sally saw Gary Neylands dancing with one of Carruth Wade's daughters, and her thoughts were suddenly cynical. Was Gary thinking of the loan he expected to get from her father, while he was dancing with the daughter?

Mrs. Boyce and Jeff Rainey danced past them and Sally heard Jeff's jolly voice and her mother's rather unwilling laughter. Mrs. Boyce had intended to come to Carol's party in Walter's car, but Jeff had arrived at the house and demanded that both Mr. and Mrs. Boyce should accompany him. Mrs. Boyce had refused coldly for herself, had declared angrily that her husband was too sick to go. But Sylvester Boyce had come stamping down the stairs, ignoring his wife's protests, and the three of them had left in Jeff's car. Sally thought fretfully, "Jeff Rainey is a stubborn young man. He apparently doesn't know the meaning of the word, 'no.'"

"Happy, darling?" Walter whispered in her ear.

"Yes," Sally replied without enthusiasm, and watched Carruth Wade dancing with Mrs. Putnam, a stout little woman whose great pride was not the fortune her husband had left her but the fact that her currant jelly had taken prizes in county fairs. Sally's thoughts were angry; "It's a crazy world and getting crazier every minute!" Her eyes strayed to her father, and her anger gave way to a feeling of profound gratitude. Sylvester Boyce was seated in a corner, watching the dancers with evident enjoyment. His expression said that he was amazed at finding himself here, but that he had again found life worth living.

Sally danced next with Gary Neylands and he was his usual suave and confident self.

"I understand that you turned my real estate man over to Jeff Rainey and that Jeff sold him a Duluth." Gary laughed softly. "I understand why you did it."

His understanding irritated her. These men who were never at a loss about anything!

"You made it impossible for me to sell him, Gary." They circled the room before Gary spoke again. "Are you happy, Sally?"

Sally wished angrily that people wouldn't ask such idiotic questions. Couldn't they see that she was happy? Weren't all girls happy when they were about to marry the men they loved?

"Very happy!" she said sharply.

"You look unhappy and it hurts me," Gary said gently. The he asked. "Can't you see that you no longer love Walter?"

It seemed to Sally that she had borne enough of his insinuations. Her angry eyes met his squarely. "Perhaps you think that I love you!" she snapped, and saw a grayness about his stiffly smiling mouth.

"I'm sure that you don't," he said easily. "But I'm equally sure that you could learn to love me."

"Your conceit is amazing!" she flared.

The music died but Gary held her for a moment longer. His voice was very firm. "You shall not marry Walter, Sally. You are going to marry me."

Sally felt a shiver of fear before the flame of determination burning in Gary's eyes. He sounded so sure. Frowning, she turned away from him and bumped into Carruth Wade.

Wade smiled at her. "I am very pleased with my Duluth, Sally." His eyes twinkled at her. "That compliment should entitle me to a dance, don't you think?"

Sally said that it did, but she couldn't pretend to be pleased with Carruth Wade, for she remembered his ridiculous assertion that she was in love with a certain irritating person whose ideas she had explained to Wade.

"I was surprised to see your father here tonight," Wade was saying. "Why didn't you tell me that he was so much improved?"

"I didn't know it myself," Sally replied, and found, as the music started again, that Wade danced well for a man his size and weight.

"Is your father making any plans for the future?" he asked.

Sally felt resentful. Had he forgotten so quickly what she had told him in his office? "I told you Dad's plans the other day," she reminded him, and his eyes widened a little.

"Yes, I remember now. He's going to promote the ideas of that boy you're in love with."

"Don't you know the reason for this party?" Sally asked coldly.

Wade shook his head. "My daughter didn't tell me."

"I am to be married to Walter Norris next week," she said stiffly. "Jeff Rainey is the young man with the ideas."

It seemed very necessary suddenly that she should convince him that she didn't love Jeff, and so, when that dance ended, she led Wade to Jeff and made the introduction. She tried to show Wade by her chilly manner just how mistaken he had been. Jeff's manner puzzled her. She had expected him to be overjoyed at meeting such an important man as Wade, but he showed only a casual interest.

"So you are the young man with the ideas?" Wade smiled.

"Some of my ideas are pretty good," Jeff admitted. "Some of them are worthless."

Sally felt like pinching him. She had given him a chance to interest Wade, but he had no better sense than to admit that some of his ideas were worthless!

"Sally was telling me about your scheme," Wade said, obviously puzzled. "I might be able to handle part of the financing."

Jeff Rainey had difficulty in suppressing a yawn. "You'll have to see Mr. Boyce about that," he said coolly.

The orchestra was playing again, and Jeff nodded to Wade and took Sally in his arms. "What are you trembling about?" he asked.

"I think I could kill you with a great deal of pleasure," Sally snapped.

"That's a good sign," Jeff said complacently. He released her, and took her hand and led her toward a door. He smiled down at her. "I have something to tell you and a certain privacy is required."

Jeff led her through a sun parlor and through another door onto a porch. And Sally went gladly. All evening she had wanted to hurt someone, and realized now that that someone was Jeff Rainey. The darkness was about them and Jeff turned to her, and she knew that he intended to kiss her. She hoped furiously that he would. Her palm itched to slap that impudent face of his. Jeff's hands were at her waist, but he was bending toward her. Sally met his eyes and the flame of anger went out, leaving another and more disturbing emotion in its place.

Jeff's lips touched hers—and her own lips melted to meet them. But it wasn't enough; she wanted to have his arms around her, crushing her against him. Jeff's lips left hers suddenly, and it was like losing a part of her own glowing body.

Jeff said gravely, "I love you, Sally." His lips quirked up. "I think, after all, I can find time to marry you next week."

Marry you—next week! The words seared through her, reminding her that she was to marry Walter next week. Reminding her that her emotions had betrayed her. One hand trembled against her tight throat.

"We— you must be mad!" she whispered.

Jeff nodded. His smile was tender. "About you, Sally."

"I hate myself," Sally choked.

Jeff's eyes were wary. "I love you enough for both of us."

Sally's anger rose and died. She couldn't slap him, couldn't blame him. Jeff hadn't held her, kissing her against her will. Her lips had gone like a homing pigeon to meet his, thirsty for his kiss, for his arms.

"It isn't true!" she wailed.

There was a pulse beating in Jeff's temples. "Don't deny my love for you," he said sternly, "or yours for me. It's cowardly."

Sally turned and fled, and panic followed her as she crossed the sun parlor, the drawing room, ignoring Walter's hail. On up the stairs she fled until she reached the door of the dressing room. She leaned against the closed door, putting a hot cheek against the cold panel, finding reality in the solid touch of the wood.

Her whisper held horror. “It isn’t true! I couldn’t bear it if it were true!”

After a moment, she entered the room but she didn’t dare look at a mirror, fearing that her face might bear some sign of her faithlessness. She thought of Walter and tears forced a way between her closed eyelids. Walter trusted her and she had betrayed him, the man she loved, her affianced husband!

The door opened suddenly and Sally dabbed at her eyes.

Louise Ives said contemptuously, “Allow me to salute the smartest girl in Avondale!”

That bitter voice turned Sally about to face the girl. And what she saw in Louise’s face made her forget her grief.

“The smartest,” Louise went on, her lips twisted, “and the cruelest! Don’t you think that you have done Walter enough damage now?” Louise asked venomously.

“Please, Louise!” Sally begged. “I don’t want to listen to you. You can say nothing of interest to me.”

Louise’s voice was quiet now. “Gary Neylands brought me to the dance tonight, Sally. We had cocktails at his apartment, which put him in a talkative mood. He told me that he was planning to market a new accessory for automobiles.”

Sally shrugged impatiently. “I don’t care to hear about it.”

Louise’s voice was like the voice of fate. “Gary told me that he bought the idea for his new accessory from Walter . . . that he paid him five thousand dollars for it.”

Sally turned swiftly to face the girl. It seemed to her that her breath was locked tightly in her chest, that she would never breathe again. “What— what do you mean, Louise?” she gasped, and saw the girl’s gleaming eyes narrow spitefully.

“Where did Walter Norris get an idea worth five thousand dollars?” Louise asked scornfully.

CHAPTER 30

A Terrified Denial

When Sally stared at her blankly, Louise Ives repeated her scornful question, "Where did Walter get an idea worth five thousand dollars?"

Sally's lungs still felt constricted, making it hard for her to breathe. She remembered Walter's secretive attitude, his refusal to disclose the source of his money. Sally wet her dry lips. "Walter didn't sell Gary an idea. You must be insane to make such a charge."

"I know when a man is telling the truth," Louise flared. "I know that Gary was telling the truth when he said that he paid Walter five thousand dollars for an idea."

Terror gripped Sally—and left her just as quickly.

"I don't believe it," she said flatly. "But there is no reason why Walter shouldn't sell Gary an idea."

Louise's eyes sparkled contemptuously. "I know Walter too well. He never had an idea in his life. Certainly not one worth that much money."

"Are you insinuating that Walter did something dishonest?" Sally asked angrily.

Louise nodded. "But not of his own volition. Simply because you made him do it."

Sally rose to her feet, trembling. "You are insane, Louise."

"You and your father are using Walter for your own ends," Louise charged furiously.

"Meaning what?" Sally snapped.

"You've been very friendly with Jeff Rainey lately, haven't you?" Louise sneered.

That name stopped Sally's heart, made it hard to speak. "Yes, I— I've been friendly with him," she admitted in a shaken voice.

"Which makes it profitable for you and your father," Louise gibed, "but pretty hard on Jeff."

"Go on," Sally ordered, when Louise hesitated.

"You know more about it than I do," Louise said uneasily.

"I thought you were bluffing," Sally said angrily.

Louise's eyes were thoughtful; they brightened suddenly. "I think I understand everything now. You and your father persuaded Jeff to explain his ideas to you. Then you use Walter as your cat's-paw in selling them to Gary Neylands. It's a clever plan for you and your father, but dangerous for Walter."

Sally's brain felt like ice. Louise was talking madness, but she could not doubt her sincerity, could no doubt that Louise meant what she said.

"My father and Jeff are going into business together," Sally said quietly. "My father believes that Jeff's ideas are worth a fortune. He'd be insane to sell them for such a paltry sum."

Louise's red lips curved in a sneer. "Five thousand dollars is a large sum for one small idea. When you've sold all of Jeff's ideas, the Boyces should be wealthy again."

"Stop—"

"And if anything goes wrong," Louise continued stubbornly, "Walter will go to prison, while you and your father go free."

Sally's thoughts were filled suddenly with Gary Neylands and his declaration that she should not marry Walter. Had Gary related this mad story to Louise, knowing that Louise would tell her about it? And hoping that she, Sally, would suspect Walter of something of which he was innocent? And jilt him?

"It won't do, Louise," Sally said calmly. "I believe I understand the reason behind what you have said. Both you and Gary want me to doubt Walter, but I don't and I never will."

Louise's eyes were steady. "I have only one reason, Sally. I love Walter and I want to save him from prison. I don't intend to stand quietly by and allow you to ruin him."

"Have you forgotten that I am to marry Walter next week?" Sally asked.

"I don't believe that you intend to marry him." A crafty look crept into Louise's eyes. "Will you deny that you have told Walter about Jeff's ideas?"

"Of course—" Sally began, and stopped as a certain picture formed in her mind. She saw herself and Walter the night of Gary's dinner, heard herself defending them, explaining proudly Jeff's idea for a radiator and gas tank cap. She remembered, shuddering, Walter had asked her recently if Jeff was having any more of his funny ideas. Remembering that she had come to Jeff's defense again, explaining to Walter Jeff's idea for parking cars."

Louise Ives' voice brought her back to reality. "Your expression tells me that you have told Walter about Jeff's ideas."

For the second time that night, Sally's thoughts uttered a terrified denial. It isn't true! I couldn't bear it if it were true! Her thoughts steadied suddenly. If she were to remain sane, she must keep a tight grip on the love and trust she had for Walter. Losing these, everything was lost. She snatched eagerly at an explanation that occurred to her suddenly. "What makes you think that Walter is incapable of inventing something worth five thousand dollars?" she asked sharply.

"Do you think that he is?" Louise sneered.

On a trembling voice, Sally gave the lie to her own doubts. "I do," she said.

Louise laughed. "I don't, and you don't, and he didn't."

"Anyway, you don't know that Walter sold Gary an idea," Sally said angrily. "If Gary owns one of Jeff's ideas, it's possible that Jeff sold it to him." But she knew, as she spoke, that it wasn't true. No, Jeff despised Gary and distrusted him and not for any amount of money would he do business with him. And she knew that Jeff would not betray her father; he just wasn't capable of doing such a thing.

"I only know what Gary told me, and so I can't be sure," Louise conceded suddenly. "But I will be sure before the night is over. I am going to ask Jeff."

Sally was sick at heart, but she took advantage of what appeared to be a small gain. "Did Gary tell you what the idea was?" Sally asked, and regretted the question instantly.

Louise's face brightened. "Yes, he did. It's an idea for a radiator and gas tank cap." She turned toward the door. "I'm going to have a talk with Jeff Rainey."

Sally's blind eyes didn't see the girl go; her deaf ears didn't hear the door open and close. She was alone in a whirling void, seeing the grim face of ruin, hearing the crash of her hopes. Jeff Rainey loved her and she had betrayed him.

"Don't deny my love for you!" he had said sternly.

Her spinning thoughts clicked suddenly to a stop. "It isn't true," she said aloud, and said it again and again as certain possibilities occurred to her. Perhaps Jeff had sold the idea to Gary. Perhaps it wasn't the same idea at all. Perhaps Gary's own research department had invented an improved radiator and gas tank cap. Perhaps Gary had bought such a device from some unknown person. Perhaps Walter could explain the source of his $5000.

By the time Sally had reached the drawing room again, she had thought of a dozen credible explanations for what Louise had told her and each of them exonerated Walter. Dancing with Walter, a little later, Sally held her tongue in check. She was feverishly anxious to question him, but this was neither the time nor the place.

"You were gone a long time," Walter said playfully. "Thought maybe you had eloped with someone else."

Sally watched his face as she replied, "I was in the dressing room, talking to Louise Ives."

Walter looked puzzled, but showed no other emotion. "Didn't know you like her enough to talk so long, Sally."

Past his shoulder, Sally saw Jeff Rainey dancing with Carol Putnam, and a shiver passed over her. Had Louise talked to him yet, repeating Gary's story? Jeff's eyes met hers, and she felt a shock of relief. The tender light in his eyes told her that Louise had not seen him.

The music ended and Jeff came to claim a dance; and Walter moved away, muttering.

"I don't want to dance now," Sally said quietly. She didn't look at Jeff, but his amusement was evident in his voice.

"Shall we return to the porch, Sally?"

Sally went rigid. "You— you received your answer, Jeff."

Jeff's voice was very gentle. "So I did. Your lips gave me a silent, but very convincing, answer."

Sally wondered if her numb lips could form words, and found, surprisingly enough, that they could. She even found that she could laugh, though the sound seemed blended with a sob. "Every girl is entitled to a silly moment, Jeff," she said lightly. "I had mine with you tonight. That moment will never repeat itself."

Jeff said for the second time that night, and just as sternly, "Don't deny my love for you, or yours for me, Sally."

"I do deny it," Sally whispered huskily.

"You have a kiss-shaped mouth," Jeff teased. "I've felt its attraction from the first . . . as you may have noticed."

Sally's shoulders lifted tensely. "Will you excuse me, Jeff? I want to speak to my father."

Jeff's gently mocking whisper floated after her: *Coward! Lovely little coward.*

Sally was standing by her father, a few minutes later, when she saw Louise speak to Jeff—saw them disappear through a door.

~ ~ ~

Seated beside Walter in his roadster, Sally stared into the night and admitted that she was a coward. Yes, she was afraid to tell Walter of the suspicion that tortured her, was afraid of what he might say in reply. Was afraid that her love for him, her trust in him, might turn to contempt and loathing. A shiver rippled over her.

"Are you cold darling?" Walter asked, smiling. "Maybe you'd better snuggle up against my shoulder."

Sally tried to speak, but her tight throat made it impossible, and not until they were parked before her house did she muster up enough courage to make a beginning.

"I heard something tonight, Walter." She swallowed painfully. "Something that made me afraid."

Walter was amused. "Has someone been scaring my baby, and at her own party?"

He made to take her in his arms, but Sally fended him off. "I heard that Gary Neylands is planning to manufacture a new automobile accessory, Walter."

Her eyes searched his face, but it was too dark to detect varying shades of emotion. Did his scowl denote curiosity—or guilt? Did his voice tremble—or was it her imagination.

"I believe that Gary is planning to do that," he said, and laughed a little. "Have you any objections, darling?"

CHAPTER 31

Stolen Device

Sally felt a surge of relief. Surely, Walter couldn't be so calm if he were guilty of selling Jeff's idea to Gary Neylands. She remembered suddenly that he didn't know the source of her information. "Louise Ives told me about it," Sally said, and found it impossible to repeat the terrible things Louise had said.

Walter's voice was still calm. "Just what did Louise tell you?"

Sally looked away from him, but that didn't make it any easier. No, she couldn't tell him. "I— I think you had better ask her, Walter." What she had said was too—dreadful!

Walter was silent for some moments, and it seemed to Sally that his breathing had quickened.

"Tell me, Sally," he ordered. "You've started this and you must finish it."

His hand closed about one of hers tightly, hurting her. But the physical pain was a relief. "I can't tell you," her whisper wailed.

Walter's voice was grim, "Tell me, Sally."

"She— she said Gary bought the idea from you," Sally began and bit her quivering lip, waiting breathlessly for him to speak, not daring to look at him, terribly afraid of what his face might reveal.

"Let us assume that this is true," Walter said evenly. "What does it prove?"

Sally was staring at the radiator cap of his roadster. She looked away from it, shivering.

"Is— is it true, Walter?"

"What else did Louise say?" Walter evaded.

"That Dad and I were stealing Jeff's ideas. That we were turning them over to you. That you were selling them to Gary." Sally's voice failed her then and she sank back into her seat.

Walter laughed. "Since you know that it is false, what are you worrying about?"

"Gary told Louise that he paid you five thousand dollars for the idea . . . an idea for a radiator and gas tank cap." It seemed to Sally that years passed before Walter's voice sounded again, and then it was the voice of a stranger.

"Did you believe her, Sally?"

Sally was stirred to anger by his question. "Don't question me, Walter. You are the one who is accused. You must prove that you are innocent."

"Do you realize that Louise is in love with me?" Walter snapped. "Or are you blind?"

"I'm not blind."

"Then you should understand her motive, which is based on jealousy. She is trying to raise doubts in your mind, so that you will refuse to marry me."

It sounded logical, Sally thought despairingly. But it didn't explain anything. "Where did you get that five thousand dollars, Walter?"

"Do we have to go into that again?" Walter growled.

"You will tell me now," Sally said quietly, "or we will never see each other again."

The lights of a passing car illuminated his face, revealed an expression that terrified her. His face was the picture of guilt.

"I— I wanted you to be proud of me," Walter stammered.

Sally braced herself for the confession that would bring to an end her love, her trust, her life.

"I wanted you to think that I was smart enough to make that much money," Walter said in a shamed voice. "I didn't want you to know that I inherited it from an uncle of mine who died recently."

Sally thought she was going to faint. She had been prepared for the worst, and her relief was hardly bearable. "You— you inherited it!"

"From my mother's brother, who died in California."

"And you didn't get the money from Gary!" Sally cried.

"Did Gary say that I did?" Walter growled.

"He told Louise that."

"How do you know that he did?"

"She— she said so."

Walter's voice was shaken. "You doubted my honesty, simply because a jealous girl wanted you to!"

Sally couldn't deny it. Walter was being honest with her; she must be the same with him. "I did doubt you, Walter. I'm sorry—"

His sarcastic voice cut her off. "For all I know, Gary may own one of Jeff's ideas."

Sally looked at him quickly, startled. "What do you mean?"

"Perhaps one of Gary's own men perfected a similar device. It's possible, isn't it?"

Sally nodded soberly. "Yes, it's possible."

"It's also possible that Jeff sold the idea to Gary."

Sally shook her head. "That isn't possible. Jeff despises him. He wouldn't sell Gary an idea for any amount of money."

"Are you in Jeff's confidence?" Walter said with ominous quietness.

"Enough to know that Jeff wouldn't sell Gary an idea."

Walter's voice showed that he was stung. "If Gary has one of Jeff's ideas, there is still another possible explanation."

Sally stared at him for a moment, then her brain caught on fire.

"Don't you dare insinuate that I betrayed Jeff Rainey."

"You insinuated that I did," Walter snarled. "However, I wasn't referring to you."

Sally felt confused. Did he mean that Jeff had confided in someone else, and that this unknown person had betrayed him?

"I can't forget that I told you about Jeff's ideas," she said dully, "and that Gary now owns one of them, or one like it."

"I can only repeat that I had nothing to do with it," Walter said stiffly.

Sally opened the door and slipped to the curb. "It isn't enough to be innocent, Walter. We must prove that you are."

"It's quite enough for me!" Walter snapped. "You father pretends to be innocent in regard to the bank, but he isn't trying to prove it. So why should I?"

He threw the car into gear and it jerked away from the curb. Sally stared after it. Her father! Had Walter dared to mean her father when saying that someone else might have betrayed Jeff?

~ ~ ~

In her bedroom, Sally sank into a chair, stared at the wall, and tried to think. And found that thinking was painful. Presently she heard a car stop before the house, heard the front door open, and the voice of her father and mother.

A few minutes later Mr. Boyce appeared in the door of her bedroom, sank into a chair facing her.

"Did Carol's party tire you Dad?" she asked gently, tying to smile, and failing.

His shaggy brows were knitted in a frown. "I'm puzzled."

Sally remembered then that Jeff had taken him and her mother to Carol's party. "Did Jeff bring you home, Dad?"

Mr. Boyce nodded. "Jeff isn't acting like himself, Sally."

Sally looked away from him, shivering, remembering Louise's declaration that she would question Jeff before the night was out. Her thoughts pictured Louise and Jeff as they had disappeared from the drawing room. It seemed to her that she could see the changing expression in Jeff's face as he listened to Louise's charge, going from bewilderment to incredulity to belief to—fury. She thought sickly, "He will hate me now . . . hate me . . . hate me!"

She asked in a dull voice, "How did Jeff act?"

"He acted like he was angry. Hardly gave me a civil goodnight." Mr. Boyce laughed uncomfortably. "Jeff didn't act like the good-natured boy I've known so long."

Sally's thoughts moved with painful clarity. Jeff had explained his ideas to her father and herself, trusting them with the things that were his life. And she, Sally, in a silly effort to defend him, had given Jeff's ideas to Walter, whom she loved and trusted. But now Gary Neylands had one of Jeff's ideas—and Jeff didn't act quite like himself.

Mr. Boyce was saying, "I can't imagine what is wrong with Jeff. I told him that everything was going well."

She laughed and the strange, choked sound brought her father to her side, peering anxiously down at her.

"Has something happened, Sally?"

She was able to tell him in a moment, everything that had happened that night. His face turned slowly white during the telling.

"You told Walter about Jeff's ideas?" Mr. Boyce gasped when she had finished.

"I told him," she said in a stricken voice.

Sylvester Boyce sank into his chair again, staring at Sally with incredulous eyes. "Why?"

Sally searched her heart for an answer to this simple question, and found the answer confusing, even to herself. "Walter sneered at Jeff's ideas. I— I just had a crazy impulse to defend Jeff. I thought his ideas were wonderful, and it made me angry to hear them disparaged."

"I should have warned you," Mr. Boyce said in a dead voice. "It just didn't occur to me that you would repeat anything Jeff said to either of us."

Sally cried, "Jeff should have kept his ideas to himself."

"Jeff told his ideas deliberately to two people . . . to Philip Ulmer and myself. This is one of the means inventors use to protect their ideas. In case of dispute, they are able to prove priority by two reputable witnesses."

Sally's hopes soared dizzily. "Then Jeff can force Gary to abandon the idea?"

Mr. Boyce laughed but there was no humor in the sound. "I imagine Gary will be able to produce two of his men, who will swear that they had the same idea before Jeff did."

"But Jeff could sue Gary," Sally cried, clinging tenaciously to her hope.

"Jeff can do that, all right," Mr. Boyce agreed dully. "But almost anything can happen in a suit of that kind. Gary might even charge Jeff with stealing the idea and get a favorable verdict."

Sally returned to her original belief—the only one that made it possible to go on living.

"I don't believe that Walter did this, Dad."

Mr. Boyce rose to his feet, and it seemed to Sally that he had aged five years in the last five minutes.

"I'm certain that Walter did it," he said huskily, lips trembling. "Which means that I shall lose my one chance to recoup my fortunes and to remove the stain from my reputation."

"But Walter didn't do it!" Sally choked. "He inherited that five thousand dollars from his mother's brother, who died recently in California."

"I grew up in the same block with Walter's mother," her father said, turning unsteadily toward the door. "Walter's mother was an only child."

CHAPTER 32

Rivals

When Sally awoke the next morning, memories of last night rushed in and she got quickly out of bed. Dressing, she pictured her father lying in his room, staring at the ceiling, filled with despair because he had lost his one chance to rehabilitate himself.

"Because of me!" she whispered, and felt her heart constrict.

Going down the hall, she came to a stop before his door. Perhaps she might be able to say something to encourage him. She rapped softly on his door.

"Come in!"

Sally opened the door and her eyes went to the bed, but her father wasn't there. Then she saw him standing by a window, fully dressed.

"I thought you'd be in bed, Dad."

"It's morning, isn't it!" Sylvester Boyce snapped. "Why the devil should I be in bed?"

Sally went to him, and he put an arm about her, and she leaned her head against him, fighting the tears. "I can never forgive myself, Dad."

"You didn't realize what you were doing, dear."

"I just can't believe that Walter did such a thing," she said in a choked voice.

"I'm afraid that I do believe it," Mr. Boyce said. "Which means that we must get busy." He looked away from her. "Jeff will never trust either of us again, but we must try to recover his idea."

"Yes, we must do that," Sally agreed soberly. "But first we must find out if it is his idea. I am going to visit Gary Neylands today."

"I'm going down town today," Mr. Boyce said worriedly. "But I don't know what I'll do."

"You aren't well enough to go down town," Sally protested.

Mr. Boyce gave her a frowning glance. "I've taken it lying down much too long. I'm on my feet from now on . . . fighting. Thanks to Jeff Rainey."

Sally closed her eyes, while her thoughts added something to her father's remark, "Thanks to Jeff Rainey, whom I have betrayed!"

~ ~ ~

Sally walked around the block three times that morning before she could force her reluctant feet to enter the Ulmer Motor Sales Company. She had to see Jeff, had to tell him that she, not her father, had betrayed his confidence, but she dreaded it more than she had thought it possible to dread anything.

Philip Ulmer looked up at her as she entered his office. His smiling face told her that he knew nothing about her trouble.

"I'd like to have you sell three or four Duluths today, Sally," he said genially.

"I'll try," Sally replied, then asked, "Where is Jeff?"

Ulmer grinned at her. "I don't believe I'll tell you. You look dangerous this morning."

"I must see him."

"Jeff has left town," Ulmer told her.

Sally's heart stopped beating. "Jeff has left town? What do you mean?"

"Jeff went to Riverdale to see a prospect. He should be back late this afternoon."

Sally's heart began beating again. She had been a fool to think that Jeff would run away; he wasn't the sort who ran from trouble. And heard her thoughts declare, "He hates you now!"

Sally went to the telephone in the display room and called Gary Neylands' office. "I want to see you this morning, Gary."

"My time is yours, Sally," Gary said easily. "Come whenever you like."

"I'll be there in twenty minutes."

~ ~ ~

Seated in Gary's office, staring at his handsome face, Sally had a queer feeling that she was here because he had willed it. Certainly his face showed no surprise at seeing her.

"I was thinking of you when you telephoned," he said soberly.

Sally was still gripped by that strange feeling. "Did you expect to see me, Gary?"

Gary's eyebrows lifted a little. "I wonder."

"Do you know why I came?"

"Of course I know, Sally. You came to tell me that you have decided not to marry Walter."

It seemed to her that his remark was an admission of his guilty knowledge, but she asked quietly, "Is there any reason why I shouldn't marry him, Gary?"

Gary studied her face for a moment, then nodded. "Because you don't love him, Sally."

He had slipped easily out of her net, and she was angry. "I do love him," she declared.

"If you love anyone," Gary said, his face darkening, "it's Jeff Rainey." His voice trembled with his contempt. "I have never thought of Walter as a rival."

Sally stared at him with wide eyes, believing that she was seeing the real Gary Neylands for the first time. And finding that she was afraid of the real Gary Neylands.

"Did you buy an idea from Walter?" she asked. And waited, hardly breathing, for his reply, which was slow in coming.

"I did!"

Sally went on staring at him. She had expected and angry denial—at least an evasion. But he was calmly admitting it, calmly bringing to an end everything that mattered to her. "It can't be true," she gasped, and saw that his eyes were guarded as if opaque shutters had dropped before them.

Gary asked, "Is there any reason why I shouldn't buy an idea from Walter?"

"Not," Sally said in a stricken voice, "if it was really his idea."

Gary's guarded eyes told her nothing; but his brows raised as if he were puzzled. "Are you trying to tell me that it wasn't his idea, Sally?"

His question gave her the right to hope a little longer. "What was the idea, Gary?"

Gary explained it briefly. And Sally turned cold as she listened. It was no longer possible to doubt that it was the same device Jeff had explained to her and her father. The same device that she, in turn, had explained to Walter. The same improved radiator and gas tank cap. Her self-loathing turned suddenly to loathing for Gary.

"How could you do such a contemptible thing, Gary!"

Gary sounded genuinely amazed. "What contemptible thing have I done, Sally?"

"Buying that idea from Walter!" she flared.

Gary's shoulders lifted. "You are talking in riddles, Sally. You will have to be more explicit."

Sally glared at him. "Are you trying to tell me that you don't know where Walter got the idea?"

Gary's lips tightened. "Walter came to me with a splendid idea for an improved accessory and I bought it, paying him five thousand dollars. It was a simple business deal, Sally."

"I gave Walter the idea," Sally whipped out.

"You!"

"Jeff Rainey explained the device to my father and myself, and I told Walter about it." She expected him to show consternation, but he merely shrugged again.

"I bought the idea in good faith, Sally. Surely you can see my side of the affair."

"Didn't you know that it was Jeff's idea?"

"But how could I?" Gary begged, hands spread. "Jeff doesn't take me into his confidence."

Sally sighed hopelessly, remembering Jeff's warning about Gary Neylands. "Don't underestimate him, Sally. Gary knows how to get what he wants."

She felt again that she rested in the palm of a giant hand, whose steel fingers were closing in on her. Felt that those cruel fingers were about to snap shut. "You must have known!" she charged angrily.

"I didn't," Gary said blandly. "But if it is really Jeff's idea, I suppose he has it patented."

"He has no patent on the idea," Sally said dully. "He's still working on it, trying to perfect it."

There was a teasing light in Gary's eyes. "Perhaps Jeff stole the idea from Walter." That teasing light left his eyes, leaving them opaque again. "Anyway, the idea now belongs to me and I am taking steps to patent it."

"You can't do that!" she said desperately. "It's theft."

Gary's teeth clicked together. "It isn't theft to buy a good idea in good faith from the person who is the rightful owner, unless someone can prove the opposite."

"But Walter isn't the rightful owner, Gary!" she cried.

Gary smiled faintly. "I prefer to believe that the idea did belong to Walter. You see, I expect to make quite a lot of money out of the device."

Sally's thoughts churned furiously. There was a question she wanted to ask, but dreaded asking because the answer would prove beyond doubt that Walter was guilty. But it had to be asked. "Can you prove to me that Walter sold you this idea, Gary?"

Gary summoned his secretary, and a few minutes later the girl laid a paper and a canceled check on his desk. He handed them to Sally.

Sally looked at the check first and saw that it was made out to Walter in the amount of $5,000. On the back, Walter had endorsed his name, in his small, precise handwriting. But even with this evidence before her, Sally clung to her hopes. She picked up the other paper. It held mechanical drawings of the device Jeff had described to her; and on the same paper was typed a detailed description of the device. At the bottom, Walter had signed a sworn statement before a notary.

"I have a bill of sale from Walter." Gary's voice penetrated the fog of her thoughts. "Would you care to see that?"

Sally didn't need to see any more, didn't need any further damning evidence. She had loved Walter, had trusted him as she trusted herself, and he had betrayed her confidence. She asked in a ragged voice, "Will you allow Walter to repay the money, so that he can return the device to its rightful owner?"

"I am its rightful owner," Gary said quietly.

Sally rose to her feet; her lips were suddenly firm. "When the case comes up in court, I shall testify that Walter got the idea from me and that I betrayed Jeff Rainey." She had expected this to crush Gary, but he was on his feet now and there was amusement in his eyes.

"You can do that," he acknowledged lightly, "but have you thought of the results of such a mad action?"

Sally shook her head. "What would the results be?"

"You will prove your fianc□ guilty of theft and swindling." Gary's mouth hardened. "You will put Walter Norris behind bars for many years to come."

CHAPTER 33

Anger and Contempt

Sally remained at Ulmer's that afternoon until the place closed, waiting for Jeff to return from his trip to Riverdale. She was ready to see him now, was braced to meet the shock of his anger and contempt.

But he didn't return, and so she went home, sat at a table with her father and mother, and made a pretense of eating. She could find no comfort in her father's gloomy face. It told her plainly that he had found no solution to their problem.

She went to his bedroom, later in the evening, wanting to comfort him if she could. He was standing at a window, staring into the darkness, his face drawn with fatigue.

"You should lie down for a while, Dad," she said gently.

Mr. Boyce shook his head, sighing. "I've spent too much time in bed already."

Sally told him what had happened during the day, about her visit to Gary Neylands and its results.

"Gary Neylands is a clever fellow," Mr. Boyce said through clenched teeth. "Damn him!"

"Very clever," Sally admitted despairingly.

Sylvester Boyce was silent for some moments, then his shoulders sagged.

"It seems to me that Gary has protected himself in every way, Sally. I don't see how we can force him to return the idea."

"Unless Walter can be persuaded to admit where he got it," Sally suggested.

"Walter isn't going to jail, just to save Jeff," Mr. Boyce said dryly.

Sally went rigid suddenly, listening to the sound of a car in the street below. Perhaps Jeff had returned to town and had decided to visit them. The car went on by and it seemed to her that some vital part of her went with it. Jeff Rainey would never come here again, bringing laughter and new life to Sylvester Boyce. Bringing something even more precious to her.

Her heart was knocking against her ribs. How could she have been so blind, so willfully blind? How could she have believed that she loved Walter, who wasn't worth loving, who wasn't even worth hating? Who was only worthy of contempt! How could she have been blind to her love for Jeff, when her lips thirsted for his, when her body hungered for the feel of his arms about her?

"You are very pale, Sally," her father said gently. "Are you feeling ill?"

Sally shook her head, unable to speak. Loving Walter had been nothing but a habit. She had felt Jeff's attraction from the first, had hated him for it. She thought dully, "I wonder how long I have loved him without knowing it?" But Jeff had known, had ordered sternly that she must not deny their love for each other.

Sally leaned her head against her father's shoulder, forced words through her constricted throat. "Did you know that I loved Jeff?"

"Jeff told me that he was going to marry you. But I knew that you didn't love him, and I'm glad now that you don't. It would be too dreadful if you did."

"I do love him," Sally whispered, and knew that it was a dreadful thing to betray the man you loved. So much more dreadful than betraying a man you merely liked because he was kind to your father. Incredibly, unbearably dreadful—not to be endured! "I can't. I can't bear it, Dad!" she said in a strangled voice.

"We must forgive ourselves," Sylvester Boyce said gently. "Jeff is only human and he will hate us when he learns what has happened. We can only hope to get the idea away from Gary and return it to Jeff. But even then, Jeff will never trust us again."

"Jeff will never trust us again," Sally agreed dully, and her thoughts carried it farther, "Never love me again."

"Speaking of ironical twists of fortune," Mr. Boyce said dryly. "Several men approached me while I was down town today, asking about Jeff's scheme. All of them wanted to invest, and among then was Adolph Gingrich."

"Then you think that you could have raised the money?"

"Without any trouble at all."

~ ~ ~

When Sally entered the display room at Ulmer's the next morning, she saw Jeff showing a sport-model Duluth to a middle-aged man and a girl who was apparently his daughter.

Jeff didn't glance at her and Sally sat down in a chair and waited. She was eager to speak to him, anxious for him to know the truth, or as much of it as she could tell him. Not, of course, that she loved him, nor that she could not bear too face the fact that his love for her had turned to hate. Sitting there with her hands locked nervously in her lap, she watched the play of expressions on his tanned face, as he pointed out the Duluth's superior qualities to his prospects. She could picture already the change, which would take place in his expression when he saw her.

She heard the man tell Jeff that he wanted to look at another car before deciding. Her breathing quickened as the couple moved toward the entrance and Jeff strode toward her. She thought for a moment that Jeff intended to go on past her to Ulmer's office, but he dropped into a chair beside her.

"Darn people who want to look at other cars before deciding on a Duluth," he complained.

Jeff's expression said that he had nothing on his mind except his failure to sell a car to the man. But Sally knew that his casualness was a mask for other emotions.

"I'd give my life to make things different, Jeff," she said quietly.

Jeff was staring straight ahead. "What things?"

"Didn't Louise tell you, Jeff?"

"Oh, that," Jeff said without interest. "Yes, she told me."

Sally waited almost impatiently for him to vent his anger and contempt on her. And when he remained silent, she felt a deep bewilderment. "I want to tell you the truth about it, Jeff."

"Go ahead," Jeff said indifferently.

But Sally was gripped by a feeling of hopelessness. She was remembering that she had asked Jeff to continue his visits to her father. No doubt, Jeff believed now that she had had an ulterior motive for that request—believed that she had wanted a chance to get more of his ideas to turn over to Walter.

"I want you to know," she said huskily, "that my father had nothing to do with it."

Jeff lit a cigarette, blew a smoke ring at the ceiling. "Has anyone accused your father?"

Sally studied his expressionless face and found nothing either to dismay or encourage her. "I am afraid that you might suspect him, Jeff. I want you to know that I gave the idea to Walter, and that dad knew nothing about it."

"Why did you do that, Sally?"

Sally swallowed. "I loved and trusted him."

"Past tense?"

"Past tense," Sally said quietly. Yes, ages ago she had loved and trusted a man blindly, willfully. Had been too foolish to know the difference between love and habit. "I gave him another idea of yours, Jeff. The device for parking cars."

"I don't imagine he sold that one to Gary."

"But he will, Jeff."

Jeff scowled. "Gary Neylands isn't a fool! He knows that that device would cost more than the car itself. I was just kidding about that one."

"But the other idea was worth lots of money?" she asked.

"The other idea," Jeff said coolly, "was worth lots of money."

"You— you don't seem concerned about it," she said fretfully.

"Why should I be? I have lots of ideas, with more on the way. One idea, more or less, makes little difference."

"Then you don't intend to do anything about it?"

Jeff glanced at her for the first time, and his mouth was grim. "I intend to get paid for the idea."

"But you can't make Gary pay you for it," Sally cried.

"Gary will pay me for it," Jeff growled.

"But how?"

Jeff's grimness was shot with a trace of his old humor. "I have always felt that Gary was too pretty, and I've always wanted to do something about it. As soon as I find time, I shall have a private session with him and exact payment for my idea."

Sally's whisper trembled. "You don't mean that you will kill him!"

"I'm not a killer," Jeff said quietly. "I merely intend to put a permanent wave in his nose, extract a few of his teeth without benefit of gas, change the color of his eyes."

"But he will have you put in jail," Sally wailed.

Jeff sighed. "We must pay for our pleasures." He rose to his feet. "You'll have to excuse me, Sally. I have a date to demonstrate a Duluth."

"But what are you going to do about recovering your idea?" Sally asked, almost in tears.

"You gave it away, Sally. It's up to you to get it back."

Watching him go, she knew that he was right, knew that she must find a way to recover the idea. She went to the telephone and called the plant and asked for Walter. When he answered, she told him that she must see him as soon as possible, and he agreed to see her during his lunch hour, though he sounded unwilling.

"Shall we go somewhere and get a bite to eat?" Walter asked, as they drove away from the plant that noon.

Sally shook her head. Her first glimpse of his face had answered her most important question. He had avoided her eyes, while a guilty color had risen to his cheeks. She drove the car into a side street, and parked at the curb and turned to him. "You lied to me about the source of the five thousand dollars!"

Walter gave her a scowling glance. "What if I did? You refused to marry me because I wasn't making enough money. What I did, I did for you, Sally."

Sally controlled her anger. "You must return that money to Gary. We can't let Jeff lose his idea."

"You want me to sentence myself to prison?" he sneered.

"If you won't confess, then I will," Sally said angrily. "I'll tell the truth, when the case goes to court."

"If you do that," Walter snarled, "I'll confess that you, your father, and myself, conspired together to steal Jeff's ideas."

"But Dad had nothing to do with it!" Sally cried.

Walter shrugged, grinning. "It's his word against mine." He met her gaze squarely. "You and I are going to be married next Tuesday . . . or I will sign a confession, incriminating you and your father."

CHAPTER 34

Mere Pawns

Walter's threat to incriminate her and her father, if she broke her engagement to him, left Sally stunned. But only for a moment.

"I'd rather die than marry you!"

The angry red drained out of Walter's face, leaving it white. "You don't mean it, Sally. You love me and you always will, no matter what happens." But he shivered before her look of loathing.

"You'd better do as I advised," Sally said huskily. "If you will return Jeff's idea, I feel sure I can persuade him not to prosecute you."

"But you can't persuade Gary," Walter growled. "If I admitted my guilt, Gary would have me in jail within the day."

"Does Gary know where you got the idea?"

"He's never said so, but I'm sure that he does," Walter said, and turned a pleading face to her. "You can't desert me now that I'm in trouble, Sally."

Sally shivered away from his groping hand, wondered sickly how she had ever been able to endure his touch. "You deserted me, Walter," she said quietly, "when you betrayed my confidence."

Walter glowered at her for a moment. "Why are you so concerned about all this? Why should it matter to you if Jeff loses one of his ideas?"

Sally met his gaze steadily. "Because I love him."

"You loved me yesterday," Walter sneered.

"I pitied you and thought it was love. I don't pity Jeff, so there's nothing to cloud my reasoning."

"Loving Jeff won't get you anything," he said brutally. "You can rest assured that he despises you for giving me his idea."

"Yes, I suppose he does."

"Have you told him that you love him?" Walter asked, scowling.

"No."

"I wouldn't, if I were you. Jeff would think that you were trying to regain his confidence, so that you could betray him again."

Sally's throat was tight. "I know that."

"Then what do you hope to gain?" Walter growled.

"I want Jeff's idea returned to him. There isn't anything I wouldn't do to accomplish that."

"If you think Gary is going to return Jeff's idea, then you are crazy," Walter snapped. "Gary has everything to gain by keeping it and nothing to gain by returning it."

Sally realized with a sinking heart that this was true, but she said firmly, "Nevertheless it must be done."

A look of self-pity touched Walter's face. "I only sold that idea to Gary so that you and I could be married, and so that I could help your father."

"You never mentioned helping Dad before," Sally said dryly.

"I didn't tell you all my plans," he said petulantly.

"You've told me enough of them," Sally said evenly, "to make me despise you as long as I live."

Walter's face turned ugly again. "If you try to injure me, don't be surprised if I protect myself."

"Meaning?"

"If you tell anyone that I sold Jeff's idea to Gary, I'll sign a confession, incriminating you and your father."

"Jeff's idea must be returned to him," Sally said doggedly, wearily.

"It won't be," Walter said, and laughed.

Sally started the engine and drove back to Gary's plant. Walter stepped out of the car and started to walk away. Sally called to him and he turned, but avoided her eyes.

"You are a weakling and this is a battle between strong people," she said quietly. "I should advise you to get Louise Ives and leave Avondale at once. Otherwise you will find yourself behind bars."

Walter shook his head, his face stubborn. "Never."

Sally's eyes held contempt. His courage was not that of a strong man, but merely that of a cornered animal. "You will, if you have a grain of sense," she snapped. "Don't you realize that Gary will throw you to the wolves if anything goes wrong?"

Walter turned and strode away and, watching him go, it seemed to Sally that the air was cleaner and fresher. It was pleasant to see him go, knowing that she need never see him again. But she had accomplished nothing, had been foolish to believe that she could accomplish anything through him.

She closed her eyes and Jeff's image was painted on her eyelids, his expression tender, his lips coming down to meet hers. Ecstasy, close to agony, flooded her. She opened her eyes, gasping. Her gaze moved over the big plant before her. Somewhere within that vast building was the clever man who had built it, the man who was accustomed to overcoming difficulties. The only man who could return Jeff's idea to its rightful owner.

She left the car and a few minutes later, she was speaking to Gary's secretary, asking to speak to him.

The girl nodded. "Mr. Neylands said that he was expecting you, Miss Boyce, and said to show you in at once."

Following the girl, Sally's lips were twisted in a bitter smile. Gary had known that she could get help nowhere else.

Gary was seated behind his desk when Sally entered the office. He rose quickly, smiling his welcome. "I've been expecting you, Sally."

Sally sank into a chair in front of the desk. "I know," she said dully.

Gary bowed, smiling. "Let me be the first to congratulate you."

"Congratulate me?"

"On breaking your engagement to Walter. It must be a great relief to you to realize that you never loved him."

Sally shivered. "Yes, I'm glad that I am no longer blind."

"Some women can be happy married to weaklings," Gary said, his eyes moving slowly over her face. "But you are not one of them. You'd have been wretched."

Sally shrugged. "I saw Walter this noon. I tried to persuade him to tell the truth, but he refused."

"You are wasting your time," Gary said easily. "Men like Walter are merely pawns in the game of life."

"And men like you?" she said dryly.

Gary smiled complacently. "We move the pawns around, for our profit and amusement."

Sally remembered that dressing room in his country house, the walls painted to represent a theater, both actors and audience—monkeys garbed as humans. The memory made her shudder. "Jeff's idea must be returned to him," she said firmly.

Gary looked at her carefully. "Why?"

"Because I love him."

Gary was suddenly grey about the mouth, but forced his lips into a smile. "You'll forget him in time, Sally."

"I'll never get over him, Gary. Never!"

His handsome face held a scowl. "Do you seriously believe that I will help the man you love, when I want you for myself?"

Sally rose, sighing. "Then I'm wasting more of my time."

Gary shook his head; he had regained his normal color. "The curtain has just raised in the last act, Sally. You must not leave until the play is ended."

Sally smiled sadly. "It seems to me that it has ended disastrously for Jeff, and myself, and my father."

"I predict a happy ending for everybody," Gary said calmly. "And since I am the author of the play—"

Sally broke in quickly, angrily. "Then you admit that you persuaded Walter to steal that idea?"

"I did nothing of the kind," Gary said sharply. "It isn't necessary to persuade a fool to be foolish. I merely took advantage of an opportunity that came my way."

Sally believed him. Yes, Gary had stood calmly by, waiting for Walter to stumble into his trap. Gary had shown cleverness in judging Walter's character—that was all.

Gary asked, "Does Jeff know what has happened to him?"

Sally nodded, and remembered with pleasure what Jeff had said about changing Gary's face. She wished passionately that she herself was strong enough to do so. "I shall always despise you, Gary," she said huskily.

Gary raised bland eyebrows. "You don't despise me, Sally. I rather think that you hate me now, but you will get over it."

"Hate is the proper word, I suppose," she admitted dully.

Gary looked pleased. "You are intelligent as well as beautiful, Sally." He nodded toward her chair. "Please sit down again and tell me exactly what you want. You can rest assured that I will give it to you."

Sally sank into the chair, staring at him, not daring to believe what she had heard.

Gary nodded, smiling. "You have but to ask for what you want, and I shall see that you get it."

"You don't mean it."

"Try me," he said briefly.

"Will you return Jeff's idea to him?"

"I had planned to do that," Gary said, and smiled at her amazed face.

"It isn't true!" she cried.

"I intend to return Jeff's idea, Sally. I intend to give your father an important position in my company when he is recovered. I intend to send Walter away and I shall not prosecute him."

Sally was resting in the palm of that giant hand again, and the fingers were closing in on her. "What do you want in return for all this?" she asked.

"You!"

Those steel fingers had snapped shut, and she was caught and there could be no escape. Yes, she could get anything she wanted, could protect the man she loved, could insure her father's future.

"I shall be very kind to you, Sally," Gary said gently. "I shall do everything possible to win your love."

Sally was on her feet, trembling. There were some things a girl couldn't do, and this was one of them. She couldn't marry a man she loathed.

"If you don't marry me," Gary said quietly, "then I shall keep Jeff's idea, and Jeff, of course, will always hate you and your father."

Sally's voice shook. "I— I'll find another way. There must be some other way."

"There is no other way," Gary told her, and then his voice became brisk," we'll be married tomorrow, Sally. It'll take me the rest of the day to clear up my work here. I have an engagement with Carruth Wade tomorrow morning at eleven, but we'll be married immediately after that."

Sally discovered in that moment that there wasn't anything a girl couldn't do, if she loved a man enough. And so she said quietly, "You win, Gary. I'll marry you tomorrow."

CHAPTER 35

Assault and Battery

Driving back to Ulmer's, Sally sought feverishly for another and more tolerable way out of her dilemma. And came slowly to the realization that Gary had built his trap skillfully and that there could be no escape. The events of the past week moved through her mind like something out of a nightmare. A week ago, she had hated Jeff Rainey, had been preparing for her marriage to Walter, stubbornly sure that she loved him. Today, she loved Jeff with a force that left her weak and trembling. But she was caught in a trap of Gary Neylands' making, and she must marry him so she could right the wrong she had done Jeff. There just wasn't any other way. This belief had become a conviction by the time she parked the car in front of Ulmer's. Gary had named his price for what he wanted, and she knew that he would accept no other. A thought occurred to her as she entered the display room and she hurried to the telephone. A few moments later, she was speaking to Louise Ives.

"What you told me at Carol's party is true," Sally said quietly, and waited for Louise's derisive laughter. But she heard a quick, frightened gasp, then Louise's trembling voice.

"What's going to happen to Walter?"

I don't know," Sally replied. "I advised him to leave town, but he refused."

Louise was shrill in giving her opinion of one Gary Neylands, but her voice quickly steadied. "Do you think I could persuade Walter to leave?" Louise asked.

"That's why I called you, Louise. I believe that you can get him to leave. I do know that he is frightened."

"The poor fool," Louise said, her voice torn between anger and pity. Then she asked, "Why did you call me, Sally?"

"I don't want Walter to go to prison," Sally said simply. "I believe that what he did was instigated by a man who is stronger and wiser than he."

"Yes. If anything goes wrong, Gary will see that Walter, not himself, pays the penalty." Louise's voice was husky with fear. "I'll get in touch with Walter at once and do everything I can to save him. I'll call you later and let you know how it turned out."

Hanging up the receiver, Sally felt a measure of relief. Despising a man for weakness, caused by a doting mother, was too much like despising him because of the color of his eyes. And she couldn't bear to see him suffer, knowing that Gary Neylands was really the guilty party.

"Ulmer's employees are supposed to keep smiling, Sally. No frowning is allowed on these premises."

Jeff's voice turned her like two strong hands on her shoulders. She saw coolness in his eyes, but his lips were faintly smiling. It made her heart pound, for she had expected never to have him smile at her again. She thought, "If I could just touch his hand, I might be able to go on living!" She said aloud, "Gary is ready to return your idea, Jeff."

"But I don't want him to return it yet," Jeff said, and the smile left his lips. "I do wish you wouldn't rush things so."

Sally felt dizzy. She had arranged for the return of something worth thousands of dollars to him—and he complained about it. "I don't understand you, Jeff."

"If Gary returns my idea now," he explained grimly, "then I'll have no excuse to put a dent in his head."

Her despair was tinged with anger. "Don't you realize that you lost a valuable invention?"

Jeff shrugged. "No reason why I should get grey-headed about it. I have enough patents already to make me wealthy."

Sally wished passionately that she could share his unconcern. Then it came to her that it wasn't genuinely that. No, his surface coolness could not blind her to the hot resentment seething within his mind. She had betrayed him—and he hated her!

Jeff asked, "How did you persuade Gary to return the idea?"

Sally looked away from him. "Does it matter?"

"Yes."

She shook her head. "I gave away your idea, but I have arranged for its return. Nothing else matters."

Jeff stared at her silently for a moment, and Sally felt that those blue eyes of his were seeing into her thoughts, seeing the truth. But he only smiled a little and turned to the telephone.

"That you, Gary?" Jeff said when the connection had been made. "This is Jeff Rainey. How would you like to buy one of my ideas?"

Sally shuddered. Had Jeff decided that he might as well sell the rest of his inventions to Gary—since he couldn't trust her and her father?

"I'll be in your office within fifteen minutes," Jeff was saying, cheerfully. He hung up the receiver, glanced at Sally.

"Please don't sell him any of your ideas," Sally begged.

Jeff looked bewildered, "Of course I shan't."

"But you just told him—"

Jeff's grin stopped her. "I merely asked Gary if he would like to buy one." His eyes narrowed thoughtfully. "I have to go to Riverdale again today, so I must run along."

"What are you going to do to Gary?" Sally asked anxiously.

His mouth went grim.

"Please don't beat him up, Jeff. He will have you put in jail. It would be too awful."

There was a faint twinkle in Jeff's eyes. "Are you casting aspersions on the Avondale jail, Sally? I'll have you know that it's one of the finest in the state."

Sally's tear-filled eyes followed him as he strode away. He was headed for trouble, and the blame for it lay with her. If he went to jail, she would have put him there.

~ ~ ~

Sally was helping her mother prepare supper that night when the telephone rang. She answered it and her heart beat faster when she heard Louise Ives' excited voice.

When she hung up the receiver, a few minutes later, she saw her father coming up the front sidewalk and went to meet him. His white, defeated face made her heart turn over. They seated themselves in a glider on the porch, and Sally took his hand and hugged it against her breast, vowing that he should not suffer because of her. "Don't worry any longer, Dad," she said gently. Jeff's idea will be returned to him tomorrow."

A little color crept into his white face. "Do you mean that Gary has agreed to return it!" he exclaimed.

Sally nodded soberly. "Yes. And Gary is going to find a splendid position for you in his business."

Mr. Boyce's mouth set like a steel trap. "Do you actually think I would work for Gary Neylands?"

Sally sighed wearily, knowing that she hadn't really believed it. Sylvester Boyce would starve before he would work for Gary.

"Gary and I are to be married tomorrow, Dad. He has an appointment with Carruth Wade at eleven, and we are to be married immediately after that."

He turned incredulous eyes to her. "You can't mean it, Sally!"

"There was no other way," she said huskily, and saw incredulity give way to a smoldering anger in his eyes.

"Does Jeff know about this, Sally?"

That name made her throat too tight for speaking; she could only shake her head.

"I was late in getting home," Mr. Boyce said gruffly, "because I went to the jail when I heard that Jeff was there, accused of assault and battery on the person of Gary Neylands."

Sally jumped to her feet. "I must go to him!"

"But Jeff wasn't in jail. Philip Ulmer had bailed him out."

Sally sank down again, glad of the darkness, which hid her tears. Jeff had been in jail and she had put him there. His score against the Boyces was mounting daily, and Gary would make sure that Jeff paid the full penalty for beating him. Her thoughts conjured up a picture of Gary, with his features rearranged as Jeff had promised, and her eyes were suddenly dry. Yes, she was glad—savagely glad—that Jeff had beaten him! In no other way could a man like Gary be bested.

"You are not going to marry Gary," Mr. Boyce said quietly.

Sally looked at him and his expression frightened her. "But I must. Surely you can see that there is no other way."

Sylvester Boyce shook his head; his mouth was grim. "We must find another way, Sally. I want Jeff's idea returned to him, too, but not at that price."

Sally's voice had a bitter humor. "Anyway, I'd rather marry Gary than Walter."

Mr. Boyce rose to his feet; his face wore a thoughtful scowl. "Did you say that Gary has an appointment with Carruth Wade tomorrow morning?"

"Yes. At eleven o'clock."

His eyes narrowed. I want you to be at Ulmer's at eleven tomorrow morning. I may want to get in touch with you."

Sally agreed, filled with a consuming pity for him. He would go on fighting until the last—but they were beaten. Gary Neylands built only escape-proof traps. She became aware of the gleam in her father's eyes, and a shiver passed over her.

"Rather than allow you to marry Gary," he said in a choked voice, "I would take the law into my own hands."

There was no mistaking his meaning and terror gripped her. She had to marry Gary to save Jeff. But if she did, Sylvester Boyce would kill Gary. No matter what she did, her father would be ruined.

~ ~ ~

Sally carried this frightening conviction with her when she went to work the next morning. She made two unsuccessful calls on prospects and returned to Ulmer's a few minutes before eleven. She was crossing the display room when she saw Jeff Rainey leave Ulmer's office and come toward her.

"No need for you to go in there," Jeff said quietly. "You father telephoned me a minute ago."

"Dad called you?" she said, puzzled, but saw that Jeff was puzzled, too.

He nodded. "He asked me to bring you to Carruth Wade's office, Sally."

Sally's heart was in her throat. Had her father gone there to meet Gary—and to carry out his threat!

"What's wrong, Sally?" Jeff asked. "You look afraid."

"I have reason to be afraid," she cried. "We must go there quickly, Jeff."

That short ride from Ulmer's to the building that housed Carruth Wade's office seemed ages long to Sally. Jeff asked no questions but she sensed his bewilderment. But she couldn't put her fear into words, couldn't tell him that she had ruined not only him but her father as well. Couldn't tell him that she expected to find that her father was a murderer!

CHAPTER 36

Confessions

When Sally and Jeff entered Carruth Wade's outer office, Mr. Boyce rose from his chair and came to meet them, putting a finger to his lips. "This is a surprise party for Gary Neylands," he whispered grimly, and glanced at Wade's secretary. "May we go in now?"

The woman nodded silently, and Sally felt numb with relief as she followed her father and Jeff. She had been so sure that her father had carried out his threat, that he had killed Gary.

When the three of them entered Wade's private office, Sally didn't at first recognize the man seated near Wade's desk. A bandage covered his nose; his eyes were puffed and discolored; his lips swollen.

"Sally!" he exclaimed, and his voice identified him as Gary Neylands. His puzzled eyes left her, went to Carruth wade. "You invited me here to discuss a loan, Mr. Wade. Why are these people here?"

"I had about decided to grant the loan," Carruth Wade said gravely. "But Sylvester Boyce has made certain charges against your character, and we must clear that up first."

Gary Neylands shot a contemptuous glance at Mr. Boyce, then he rose to his feet and nodded coldly to Wade. "I'll come back some other time," he said.

Jeff Rainey stood in front of the door leading to the outer office. His eyes moved critically over Gary's face. "It seems to me that I fell down on the job yesterday," Jeff said regretfully. "But I can make further changes in your face today."

Gary sank into his chair again, scowling. "This is an outrage!" Gary's angry glance went from Jeff to Sylvester Boyce. "Well, what do you want? I'm very busy today. I suppose Sally has told you that we are to be married this afternoon?"

Sally looked as Jeff and saw his eyes widen, saw the muscles of his neck go rigid. His glance swung to her, and his eyes were like blue ice. "So that's how you persuaded him to return my idea?"

"Yes," Sally said in a smothered voice, and saw a furious color touch his lean cheeks as he looked at Gary.

"Did you think I would allow you to marry Sally, you fool!" Jeff whipped out.

"Sally has agreed to marry me, and I shall hold her to it," Gary said disdainfully. "You have nothing to say about it."

Mr. Boyce cut in quietly, "I have something to say about it."

"Not in this city, you haven't," Gary snapped. "Sally is old enough to make her own decisions."

Sally felt suddenly very weary. This talk couldn't possibly change anything. Gary still had Jeff's idea, and he would not part with it unless she married him.

Mr. Boyce said grimly, "If you hold Sally to her promise, she will be widowed immediately following the ceremony!"

Gary glanced at Carruth Wade. "You are a witness to this threat."

Wade started. "What threat?" he asked. "Sorry, but I'm troubled with deafness at times."

Gary shrugged and looked again at Sylvester Boyce. "I don't believe you," he growled, "and even if I did, it would make no difference. Sally and I will be married today."

"Dad does mean it, Gary," Sally cried. "Please, listen to him."

Gary shook his head stubbornly. "You and I settled this matter yesterday, Sally. There is nothing further to be said."

Carruth Wade looked at Mr. Boyce. "You told me you wanted to make charges against Gary's character, Sylvester."

Mr. Boyce nodded. "Gary bought an idea for an auto accessory from Walter Norris, knowing that it belonged to Jeff Rainey."

Gary interrupted roughly. "I bought it from Walter, knowing that it belonged to him. I can prove this by Walter's sworn statement. And Walter is prepared to give oral testimony."

Sally closed her eyes despairingly. Gary had protected himself perfectly. Nothing could be proved against him. Her eyes opened suddenly. She was remembering Louise Ives' telephone call of last night. She said quickly, "Walter has left town."

"Where did he go?" Gary asked uneasily. "I told him to stay

here."

"She didn't say," Sally replied.

"She?" Gary repeated, puzzled.

"Louise Ives. They went away together last night. Louise said that they were going far away and that nobody would know their destination."

"Looks like you've lost your best witness, Gary," Wade observed.

Gary shrugged, smiling. "I still have his sworn statement, proving that the idea belongs to me. My lawyer tells me that my position is impregnable." His cold eyes fell on Jeff. "My lawyer tells me that you will pay dearly for what you did to me."

Jeff smiled contentedly. "It was worth it."

Sally sighed wearily. This talk was getting them nowhere. Gary Neylands was still master of the situation.

Mr. Boyce spoke again. "It seems that I am going to be forced to tell the truth." Carruth Wade asked, "What is the truth, Sylvester?"

Sally looked at her father, but his eyes avoided her. She saw his thin shoulders straighten.

"I want to make a full confession," he said quietly.

"Go right ahead," Carruth Wade urged cheerfully.

Mr. Boyce said firmly, "Gary Neylands, Walter Norris, and myself, conspired together to steal Jeff Rainey's ideas!"

Sally stared at him with wide eyes, too choked to protest.

"It's a lie!" Gary Neylands snarled.

Mr. Boyce looked at him blandly. "I would never have betrayed you, Gary, if you hadn't tried to marry Sally."

Gary was on his feet, glaring at the older man. "You must be insane! I don't know what you are talking about."

Mr. Boyce met his gaze squarely. "Of course you remember how you, and I, and Walter, planned to swindle Jeff."

Sally felt sick and faint. Her father's plan was clear to her. He intended to sacrifice himself to save her and Jeff.

Gary turned a red face to Carruth Wade. "It isn't true."

Wade frowned thoughtfully. "If Sylvester makes this confession in court, it will look bad for you, Gary."

"I'll make it in court," Mr. Boyce said determinedly.

"It's preposterous!" Gary cried. "No court will believe it."

Mr. Boyce's eyes sparkled sardonically. "Most of Avondale already believes that I am dishonest. They'll believe it when I admit to further dishonesty."

"You will ruin yourself," Gary said desperately.

"I'm ruined already," Mr. Boyce said quietly.

Carruth Wade cleared his throat. "It looks pretty bad for you, Gary. If Sylvester does swear to this in court, you won't have a leg to stand on."

Gary's incredulous eyes were fixed on Mr. Boyce. "You'd ruin yourself, just to ruin me?"

Mr. Boyce shrugged. "I have told the truth."

Sally watched Gary as he snatched up a telephone from the desk and called his office. She heard him instruct his secretary to get the Walter Norris papers and send them immediately to Jeff Rainey at the Ulmer Motor Sales Company. He set the phone down with a clatter.

Mr. Boyce said quietly, "You will also agree not to press charges against Jeff for the deserved licking he gave you yesterday."

Gary hesitated for a moment, while his glowing eyes moved over all of them; then he strode to the door. "You win," he snarled, and the door banged behind him.

Sally didn't believe it. Her eyes and ears had played a trick on her. Gary Neylands hadn't left here defeated; he hadn't admitted it in so many words. Miracles didn't happen nowadays.

Jeff Rainey chuckled. "I have a confession to make, too," he said. Their eyes turned to him. "I made a model of that idea the same day I thought of it. One of the mechanics at Ulmer's helped me make it. I've been using it on my car and a dozen people have seen it, which would make it impossible for anyone else to patent it."

Sally's feeling of numbness gave way to anger. Jeff might have spared her father this humiliation. Her anger died. Jeff hadn't known what they were doing. "You— you might have said so," she stammered.

Jeff grinned at her. "If I had I wouldn't have had an excuse to wallop Gary." His face became grave. "I had another reason. I wanted your father to discover that he is in fighting shape again." He turned admiring eyes to Mr. Boyce. "You have proved that you are a fighter . . . and a darned good actor."

Mr. Boyce's jaw dropped. "Didn't you believe my confession?"

"Don't be an idiot," Jeff said gently.

"This leaves me with a large amount of capital on hand," Carruth Wade complained. "The money I was planning to lend to Gary." He looked at Mr. Boyce, his eyes twinkling. "Would you mind telling me about this scheme of yours and Jeff's?"

Mr. Boyce swallowed. "Didn't you believe me, Carruth?"

"Didn't you hear Jeff tell you not to be an idiot?" Wade growled, and glanced at Sally and Jeff. "If you two will run along, Sylvester and I can get down to business."

Sally and Jeff marched silently through the outer office. They marched silently to the end of the corridor—and discovered that the elevator was at the other end. They smiled at each other.

"Who cares about elevators, anyhow?" Jeff said.

Sally didn't. She only cared that the coolness was gone from his eyes, that his smile was its old self again, that she could touch his hand if she wanted to. But it was enough, for the moment, to stand quietly beside him knowing that she had escaped from a trap and was free again. Jeff's eyes met hers and they were very blue and very deep, and she felt that she could drown in them and be glad to drown.

"I've just had a grand idea," Jeff said soberly.

Sally smiled a little. "Is it a good one, Jeff?"

"The only really good one I've ever had."

Sally saw the idea in his eyes, explained in terms of love and tenderness, and her heart swelled to receive it. "It is a grand idea, Jeff."

His eyes widened. "You know what it is?"

"Of course."

"About the license? . . . and the minister? . . . and the honeymoon? . . . and all the rest, Sally?"

"Forever and ever," Sally whispered, and let his strong arms take her and hold her, knowing that forever wouldn't be—too—long.

The End

FOUR-EYES

A Short Story

Mary Ann was nearsighted—terribly, incurably so. Without her disfiguring, thick-lensed glasses, she could not identify objects ten feet away. Yet she had fallen in love with a perfect man. She heard his voice now as they walked down the darkened theater aisle.

"There are two empty seats in this row, Mary Ann."

Turning into the row of seats, they bumped together, and Mary Ann got the impression that they had started to precede her. Yet it was unbelievable that John should have bad manners. For he was flawless.

"Swell show, isn't it?" he whispered ten minutes later.

Mary Ann nodded miserably, her gaze fixed on the silver screen where she knew, lovely Yvonne Baker and handsome Jonathan Good were enacting a love story that would make them still more famous. But without her glasses she saw only blurred, distorted images. And she didn't care to put them on. John would hate her. She knew! As a child in school the little boys had called her "four-eyes," so she was miserably aware of the masculine attitude toward such things.

Her eyes smarted with the strain and she closed them for a moment, then opened them and looked at John. Not that it was necessary to look at him to see him. His faultless profile and well-shaped head, his wide-shouldered figure, were clearly visible to her, even when her eyes were shut.

It had been like this for a lifetime, for clocks were liars. True, she had met him only the night before at May Stong's party; yet she had experienced a lifetime of happiness—and pain—during those brief hours. May Stong had introduced them.

His eyes had told her clearly, distinctly: "You are beautiful! You are the girl I have been waiting for. There has never been, and can never be, anyone but you."

And her own face, she knew, must have been aflame with the

answer: "I am glad! I, too, have waited."

And then, still wordless, she had been in his arms, and they had danced to music neither of them heard, weaving in and out among couples neither of them saw.

He had taken her home. At her door he had stood silently regarding her, his hands on her arms, his eyes telling her things that were ineffably dear. He had asked her, finally, to go to the movies with him the following night. Then he had bent swiftly, and for one ecstatic moment, his lips had told her lips what his eyes had been telling her eyes.

It was not until she had reached her own room, and was seated in front of her mirror, that she remembered her spectacles—remembered that she had not worn them all evening. Staring into the mirror at her slender rounded figure, her loose dark hair, two lovely brown eyes had stared back at her, telling her things that turned her soft lips into a bitter line. Telling her that while she was beautiful without her glasses, she was ugly with them. That only some man equally afflicted could understand and care.

And now, seated here in the darkness beside him, staring at his profile, she repeated these things to herself. She had loved and lost all within twenty-four hours. But she would not, she assured herself grimly, be a fool any longer. She opened her handbag and took out her glasses.

~ ~ ~

"It was a nice show, wasn't it?" she whispered to John.

His eyes fixed intently on the screen; he didn't answer. She put her hand on his arm and repeated her remark. He started, then his face turned to her, a half-smile on his lips. Mary Ann's heart sank as she watched his expression. The smile vanished and he stared at her, wide-eyed, for a long moment.

"Didn't know you wore glasses," he said finally; then he was looking at the screen again.

"I'm almost blind without them," she told him clearly, her eyes on his averted face. He ignored her, intent, apparently, on the picture. But Mary Ann knew better. The rest of the show was a nightmare to her.

Finally, they were standing at her door, and she was swallowing hard against the tight band about her throat. She must say goodnight—and good-bye. She must not let him know.

His hands were on her arms again and his voice was in her ears, insistent, just a little bit hoarse: "I'm glad, Mary Ann. I thought you were perfect—that I wouldn't have a chance. That you wouldn't understand. I suffer from an incurable ailment. That's why I tried to precede you to our seats, so I'd have you on my right."

She was in his arms somehow, trembling.

"You see," his lips were against her ear, "I'm stone deaf in my left ear, darling. Can't hear a thing."

He couldn't say anymore, for Mary Ann had stopped his lips in the age-old way.

The End

About the Author

R. H. Davis was born in Buchanan, Missouri, in 1897. His father was a Methodist minister, which meant the family moved often. In 1913, they relocated to Florida, and after completing a single year of high school, Davis left home.

In December 1917, Davis joined the US Army and was discharged in June 1919 as a corporal with the Twenty-Third Engineers of the Second Battalion. After leaving the army, he spent several years in Texas and Georgia, but by 1930 he was again living in Florida, where records indicate he sold advertising for a newspaper; little else is known about how he made a living.

In his lifetime, he published a short story, "Four-Eyes," and a novel, *That Boyce Girl.* It is unknown whether he completed any other works.

In 1943, Davis died suddenly at the age of forty-six.

Made in the USA
Las Vegas, NV
18 March 2022

45837203R00115